ACKNOWLEDGEMENTS

I owe many thanks to many people. First, to my wife Nancy, who has been there and put up with all my hair-brained ideas.

To my dearest friend, Patty Marsan, whose enthusiasm for the project has been so valuable to me.

To Debbie Allen who was the first person to love my story 20 years ago and gave me my first taste of opera.

To Susannah Nathan, (aka Ariel), for her spiritual connections and her help in editing.

To my wonderful parents, I love them dearly.

All of my family and friends, who, in one way or another gave me needed inspiration and support.

To Jack Crompton, a modern day renaissance man, who did my book cover, advised and encouraged me throughout this work.

To Neil Wiseman for his final edit of the book.

To all the Captains and crews I have sailed the oceans with over the last thirty years.

To the crew of the Hyannis Whale Watcher, and the Acadian Whale Watcher who shared so many memorable moments watching whales.

To Captain's Joe Miller, Joe Conway, George Blanchard for all the laughs and good times on the high seas together.

To Craig Buffinton who has offered a helping hand to me many times over the last few years.

Finally, to that higher power, who sends down that little voice that tells me such wonderful stories!

Visit the Millennium Angel Web Site at
theangelof2000.com

PUBLISHERS NOTE:

Published by Vinland Images, Cape Cod, MA
www.vinimage.com

Copyright © 2000 by Bob Wilds

Library of Congress catalog number: 00 – . . . .

PZ7. 2000 [Fic]-de21 00 . . . . ..

ISBN . . . . ; *Millennium Angel, A Novel* : contemporary fantasy.

Vinland Images printing: April 2000
0 9 8 7 6 5 4 3 2 1

CONTENTS

Nancy,

May the spirit of
the Cathedral anchor fill
you with their light & love

Bob
Whit

6-25-99

The All Knowing had finished preparing the planets and stars, leaving them to their destinies. The Earth was being readied for the plans of the All Knowing, and in order to protect this new jewel in the universe, Angels were placed as guardians of the planet. Of all planets, Earth was of particular significance. A new consciousness was about to enter the grand scheme of things: Humans.

Recognizing that these beings would need special attention throughout time, a number of Angels were sent to assist them and make sure the Earth would become a heavenly place for all. The last of these Angels was a potent light. Known as the Millennium Angel, her mission was to gather and sustain the aura of kindness and goodwill throughout the world.

The day of Angels was upon the Earth, and the All Knowing released his allies to their prospective tasks.

There was Arch Angel Michael, whose mission was to battle evil, dispel negativity, and to give courage to those in need.

Rafael was sent to work with artists and healers in the world.

Gabriel came next to deliver the Word of the All Knowing to humankind.

Uriel assumed responsibility for helping people in their spiritual endeavors.

Haniel would foster beauty, love, happiness and harmony in the world.

Raziel became the keeper of secrets and mysteries.

Auriel would oversee the unfolding of human destiny.

The All Knowing recognized the immensity of the task He gave His eight Angels, and decided the last of the Angels would lie in a deep sleep until the world would need her light. They placed her in a deep ocean cave filled with cracks allowing the warmest currents and the Sun's most powerful rays to penetrate.

The Millennium Angel's wings were colored sky blue, and when they were spread open by the current, seemed to offer a gesture of salutation to the Sun. Her long slender being lay curled in luminous light that was reflected off the rocks and thick weeds. Sea plants drifted over her gently, stroking her motionless body, helping her maintain a peaceful sleep. The sounds of water moving through the cave were subliminal lullabies that nourished her soul in its dream state.

There would come a time when the accumulated burden of darkness would need to be eased, a time for the light of the world to be renewed. Then she would be called forth and awakened by the All Knowing in the year the humans call 2000.

Until then, her fate in this world of duality and free will remained a mystery.

Chapter One

ANGELS BEWARE

All seemed to be going well for the Millennium Angel, but that was about to change dramatically. Sharp long teeth glowed in the dull morning light outside the cave. Flashes of metallic scales could be seen as small fish fled from the jaws of a ten foot barracuda. The speed and persistence of this barracuda were too much for one escaping fish that was gripped tightly in its teeth. With a few thrashes of its menacing head the prey was reduced to a few particles of flesh sinking to the sandy bottom. The rest of the school of fish found shelter at the end of a nearby cave.

The barracuda ventured cautiously into this cave, a place it had never seen before. Heedful of potential danger the barracuda moved warily. The idea of cornering and eating the school of fish dispelled any misgivings about the possible dangers of this cavern. The barracuda was confident that he was a match for almost any enemy.

As he entered the mouth of the cave and drew near the panic stricken fish a glow of light blinded him just long enough for the little fish to escape. The barracuda eyes were riveted to this glowing object. Never before had he seen anything so bright. Inching his way forward, the curious barracuda drew close to the head of the Millennium Angel.

He was awe struck. "This being is no member of the dark world," he thought.

The Angel's long soft hair still flowed with the gentle current and the weeds massaged her sleeping form. As she drifted in her world of dreams, the Millennium Angel did not know the nightmare that was beginning that could destroy the oceans of the Earth.

The barracuda was named Spikes because of his especially long and sharp fangs. Spikes knew that exposing the Angel to the Lord of Darkness would boost his status with the wicked master of the deep, the feared and dangerous one known as Kratch. Spikes made a mental map of the location of the cave and rushed off to alert Kratch of his discovery.

When Spikes was safely out of sight, the school of fish that had just escaped re-entered the cave and made a valiant effort to awaken the Millennium Angel. No matter what they did or how they tried, they could not arouse her from the deep sleep given to her by the All Knowing. The fish knew they must contact Megadon the Great White Shark, and tell him of the Angel's peril. Megadon worked with the All Knowing. Where they would find the magnificent leader was a mystery, but they knew they must. The school surfaced in a cloudless sky, and looking, an arrow shaped cloud pointed the way.

Meanwhile, Spikes had arrived at the mouth of the gloomy hole of this feared and deadly leader of the Dark World.

The home of Kratch was swarming with his many soldiers. These soldiers were barracudas like Spikes, whose reputation as killers was well known. To the living creatures of the deep the soldiers were referred to as the 'Bullycudas'. Many were the legends of the Bullycudas feeding frenzies. They were the most feared school of fish in the sea.

As Spike approached, he was immediately surrounded and bullied to the far edges of the midnight blue hole that housed Kratch. Spikes knew he must justify his visit or die. The leader of the soldiers, General Slash, ripped a small bite into the sides of Spike to increase his apprehension.

Spikes stammered to General Slash. "General, I have ah, discov ... ah ... covered the, um ..."

The General swam into Spikes. "Be quick and be clear, or die," insisted the General.

"Well sir," Spikes offered meekly. "I have discovered an Angel of great light in a cave."

All the barracudas became silent as the General twisted his head violently in review of his soldiers, casting his one good eye over them. The General's other eye had been ripped from his head when he wasn't quick enough in answering to Kratch. It made him a far more menacing presence to the soldiers. The General positioned himself nose to nose with Spikes. Drips of blood and flesh from a morning meal were still fresh in his gaping mouth as his one eye looked right through Spike's bulging pupils.

Spikes was paralyzed with fear until the General spoke. "Follow me, Spikes and you can tell Kratch of your discovery. If you are wrong, I will have the pleasure of ripping you up as my dinner." The General chuckled fiendishly.

Spikes feared the dreaded Kratch after years of hearing terrifying tales of his existence in the black hole.

Kratch was rarely ever seen by anyone but the General. The many tales of his cruelty and merciless acts of revenge were legendary. The General said precious little about Kratch's appearance, but soldiers would tell of seeing his dark and ominous shape rising early in the morning to capture unsuspecting fish. It was rumored that he would eat his own soldiers if he were hungry enough.

Those who claimed to have seen him said his body was gray and bulbous with an enormous snake like head. It was said his teeth extended a third of the length of his body, and his fin's were filled with razor sharp scales speckled white from the chipped and shattered bones of his enemies and prey. Along the edge of his mouth a scar ran deep along his face to a moon shaped eye. The scar was said to be the result of a battle in his youth with Megadon, the guardian of the Oceans of Light. Megadon was Kratch's greatest enemy. It was no secret to the Bullycudas that Kratch devoted a great deal of his day to thinking of revenge.

The General and Spikes descended into the abyss that housed Kratch. The pungent odors of dead fish filled the waters. Spikes could sense that even the General's heart was pounding with fear. As they went deeper it became quieter. There was not even the slightest movement of water. Now the most foul of smells filled the entrance to Kratch's hole. The decaying flesh littering the ocean floor could barely be seen in this dark pit.

In uncontrollable fear, Spikes began to swim back to the surface. Out of the darkness two gigantic eyes filled his escape route. The whites of the bones caught in the fins of Kratch peppered the water like shattered stars over the head of Spikes. The mighty Kratch halted Spikes in his flight. He couldn't move an inch. Kratch now hovered over Spikes, inspecting this invader of his dark, mysterious world. Spike was so paralyzed with fear that when the General urged him to speak of the Angel, he could not.

On Spikes behalf, the General told the story before the impatient Kratch could slice Spikes to ribbons with his fin's. "Honorable Lord of Darkness," the General began. "This faithful follower of the dark has come to me with news of an Angel of light in a cave. This subject before you, sir, is Spikes, who has agreed to tell us where we can find this Angel."

Kratch's eyes opened enough to light the hole sufficiently enough so they could see each other easily. Kratch's eyes were almost all white with thin purplish red cracks that led to a speck of black in his pupils. He told the

General to keep quiet, and unexpectedly, a charming side of Kratch emerged as he addressed Spikes.

"Please, my fellow follower of the Dark World, relax," Kratch urged. "Your news brings me great pleasure, and I intend to reward you handsomely. Now tell me all there is to tell of this supposed Angel."

Kratch's fearsome appearance softened slightly as Spikes began. Spikes, now bursting with importance and enthusiasm, commenced his tale of the morning hunt for fish and his chasing them into the cave. Spikes embellished the episode for effect and made his entry into the cave seem especially gutsy and brave.

When he finished, Kratch seemed truly impressed and told Spikes he knew of the cave described, and thanked him. Before Spikes accepted the thanks, Kratch spoke again. "Spikes you have proven a worthy follower in bringing this information to me, and for that, you will forever hold a special place with me."

Spikes beamed with confidence and pride.

"You may go now and the General will see to it that you are well rewarded for your service."

"Thank you Lord, it has been an honor," said Spikes as he hurriedly swam off.

"General Slash, gather up the soldiers and begin to cover the Angel's domain with coral. I want coral that will grow hard and fast, sealing the Angel in the cave for all of time. For the finishing touches I must locate the Jellyfish Wizard.

"General, send soldiers to locate the Wizard and send him to me at once. In the meantime, begin to secure the cave."

Far across the ocean Megadon was watching his son, Naw, lead the other great white sharks to the feeding grounds to gather food for the day. Megadon marveled at the leadership his cherished son now displayed as he organized and led the school of sharks off into the watery unknown.

Early on, it seemed as though Naw would never develop into the type of leader that could take over Megadon's role as the protector of the oceans. Megadon began to realize he was getting very old and he prayed that Naw would take his place as the overseer of this magnificent watery kingdom.

After all, Megadon was now thirty five million years old and he was anxious to join his Maker, the All Knowing. As soon as he felt the oceans had a new leader as worthy as he was, he planned to give his body to the sea and his soul to the heavens. Megadon was comforted and certain Naw had become a worthy successor. He intended to transfer his place of power to his son very soon.

Megadon was over fifty feet long and his mouth was still white with rows of razor sharp teeth, his skin was a light soft grey. Wrinkled skin and scars covered his back — half the dorsal fin was missing. Kratch had torn it off in one of their many confrontations. Most of Megadon's scars were the result of his battles with the evil forces of the oceans. Megadon's greatest battles were with Kratch and his soldiers.

Kratch emerged early in the morning to greet the General who had just arrived with the news of the completion of the coral prison. The General was surprised at Kratch's unusually good mood. Kratch insisted on listening to the entire story as to how they packed the coral to create a rock solid prison for the Millennium Angel.

Kratch congratulated the General and offered him a fish he had just caught that morning. That was the first time the General had ever received a gift from Kratch.

The General ate the fish with pride as his soldiers looked on, most of them seeing Kratch for the first time. None of the soldiers dared to look eye-to-eye with Kratch.

"This momentous occasion will alter the power of the Dark World for all time," Kratch assured them. "Soon we will rule all the oceans. Your work has delivered the opportunity for me to complete my life's ambition," he finished in congratulation.

The soldiers all cheered.

"Now come with me and feast on the school of fish I have caught as my way of thanking you," invited Kratch.

The soldiers were quick to head for the pile of fish that Kratch offered them. Kratch asked General Slash to wait.

"General, come," ordered Kratch. "I have marked my time wisely while you were gone."

At this, a blue neon light emerged from Kratch's hole. It was the Jellyfish Wizard. He was ten feet long and his tentacles wiggled slightly back and forth in the current. Bold oranges and neon blues came in and out of brightness as the Wizard came free from the hole. His eyes were sunken behind a viscous clear skin, while two glowing bulbs of emerald green showed bright against his large black pupils. He looked around at the gathering of Bullycudas and made a quick swinging movement in a big circle.

From the tentacles, a myriad of sparkles appeared like diamonds and in a matter of seconds burst into small fish. Multiplying before all eyes, these sparkles turned fish swam freely about, filling the waters that surrounded the Wizard. The Bullycudas instinctively went to investigate what they thought were fish and possible food.

Suddenly, the fish vanished before they could come any closer than a few feet. They had witnessed the magical powers of the Jellyfish Wizard, and his magic was no secret to either them, or Kratch. He had proven an evil and powerful ally of Kratch many times. The Wizard's illusion of fish was an old trick Kratch and the Wizard had employed many times to lure victims for their own devious pleasures. The bewilderment of the stunned Bullycudas caused the General and Kratch to laugh.

"General," Kratch called. "The Wizard has joined me here while you were at the cave. He has aided me greatly in masterminding a brilliant trap to capture Megadon's son,

Naw, and destroy Megadon forever! Come and hear the plan." Kratch motioned for the General to follow.

The Jellyfish Wizard, the General and Kratch all sank into the dark hole of Kratch's lair to plan the end of the world of Ocean Light. Kratch settled in alongside the Wizard and the discussion began.

The Jellyfish Wizard spoke first. "General, Lord Kratch and I have decided to send you to Megadon today with a challenge — one that will determine the fate of the oceans for all time. Here is what we want you to do: Megadon will no doubt wish to save this captured Angel, correct?"

"Why, yes, I suppose," said the General.

"And we know the only one worthy of his Great White Sharks is his son, Naw."

"Uh huh, that is true," replied the General.

"Then it only makes sense that Megadon would send his son to rescue this Angel. When he does, we capture him and use him to lure Megadon to us for his last battle here on Earth," finished the Wizard.

"All well and good," said the General. "But how will you know when and where to capture them?"

The Wizard turned to Kratch. "I can see why he has made the rank of General. Yes indeed General: how will we know? This is how," the Wizard blurted loudly.

The Wizard unfolded a map before the General. "This, General, is the Map of Currents. It will assure the track the rescuers must follow. We will challenge Megadon with this gauntlet of destinations. The paths eventually all lead them to Kratch. When they find him they must find a way to eliminate him," the Wizard informed the General.

"Why would we wish to place Kratch in such a position?" the General wondered.

"Believe me General, no warriors could ever penetrate this territory and survive. It is all merely an elaborate trap!"

"And what if the trap fails ..." the General mumbled.

"Let the Wizard continue," Kratch ordered.

"No matter how they proceed," the Wizard continued, "the warriors will always find themselves moved into harm's way by the strong currents; currents that will deliver our enemies into waters both unknown and dangerous. Here, look the map over General."

The Wizard pointed to the first destination in the map. "These are the Canyons of Perpetual Darkness, and it is here that I will help you and your Bullycudas stop Naw and his soldiers. But before any of us intervene in the Canyons we will first see if they successfully pass their first hurdle, the Burrows of the Giant Worms. Should they escape these demons of the deep they will then have to pass right into the Canyons where we will be waiting for them. If, under the most remote chance, they get beyond the Giant Worms and escape our efforts," the Wizard concluded, "then they will float right into the path of Tentacle the Squid."

"I hate to ask, but what if they get beyond Tentacle?" inquired the nervous General.

"Then they will meet Kratch for a final showdown. They

will have to kill our great leader with a special weapon. One in fact, that we will provide for them. This Tooth."

The Wizard leaned towards Kratch and touched a great white Tooth located just below his right flipper. Kratch winced as the Wizard touched it.

"Yes General, this Tooth! The one Megadon nearly destroyed me with one hundred years ago when I killed his only wife. It was my finest and most evil day. I took her life during Naw's first birthday. When she left his side for a moment, I came up behind her and cut her deep with my flippers and fled as she floated, wounded, to the surface.

"Megadon chased me down and we battled. He sank the Tooth just inches from my heart, and left me for dead. After days suffering on the ocean floor the Jellyfish Wizard discovered me and revived me.

"The challenge we will issue shall not be refused!" Kratch boastfully went on. "When he accepts he will soon find himself without his son or his precious universe. So, good General, if all the others fail then it will be up to me to save the Dark World of the oceans, a challenge I welcome.

"General, there is a final detail to entice Megadon. Under the conditions of this challenge, I will give up my place as the master of evil if I lose. If I win, Megadon must do the same and give his throne to me."

"Do you like the plan?" the Wizard asked.

"Yes," the General queried. "But why am I going to tell Megadon of this challenge?"

"You, General are the most competent," the Wizard

informed him. "So you will deliver this map, Tooth, and terms of the challenge to Megadon.

"Come, Kratch, let's have the Tooth," the Wizard demanded.

Kratch handed the rolled map and a note to the General. He grimaced, and with a lightning quick twist of his head he used his exceptionally long teeth to yank the Tooth from his body and winced in pain as blood gushed from his side.

Holding the blood soaked Tooth in the General's face, Kratch said, "This, my General, belongs to Megadon. This Tooth almost killed me. Now it will cost Megadon's son his life." Kratch sank slowly into his dark lair trailing a stream of blood.

General Slash then chose his five finest soldiers. With the map, the note, and special Tooth under his flipper they set off in search of Megadon.

Megadon was enjoying the reflections of light as great white sharks, the members of his army of trusted soldiers streamed by. His reverie was disturbed by urgent news. A very brave school of fish was being escorted to him as he rested on his favorite ledge. The flicker of silver scales created a shimmer of light through the water, and the shark leading the school now became visible through the blue waters.

Megadon urged the school closer as the fish began telling their tale of the ferocious and persistent barracuda.

He listened intently until they finished, and all joy fled from the heart of Megadon.

Kratch had captured the Millennium Angel.

Cheerlessly, Megadon blessed the fish and had them escorted to safety. His aged and wrinkled face was deeply troubled as Naw rushed to his father's side. Megadon unburdened himself to his son, and Naw immediately offered to undertake a rescue attempt.

"Not yet, Naw," Megadon urged. "The cave will be heavily fortified and we cannot condone the losses such a confrontation might encompass. I need time to think," he said. He swam slowly to the surface to seek the guidance of the All Knowing.

As dawn broke, ending night's grip, Megadon continued his vigil. He was in deep meditation when Naw came to report that a General Slash had come to see him.

Megadon looked in the distance to see his soldiers coming to him. One hundred ten foot high dorsal fins were breaking the water as they escorted General Slash and his soldiers to this meeting. General Slash approached Megadon as Naw positioned himself between the notorious General and his father. Naw expected trickery even though the General left his guard behind in the company of Great White Sharks.

General Slash moved slowly toward Megadon and bowed in respect. "Honorable Megadon, I bring you word of the capture of an Angel."

"We are aware of your imprisonment of this Angel,"

Megadon interrupted impatiently. "So get on with your message from Kratch."

The General was surprised by Megadon's prior knowledge of the Angel's capture. "I have a proposal for you to consider that could assure the release of the Angel. Does this interest you?" the General inquired.

"Hand it over," Naw responded sharply.

"I've been instructed to wait here for your answer," the General replied. He then handed the note, the map and Tooth to Naw to transfer to his father.

Megadon regarded the Tooth and then addressed the General. "Tell me General, did it pain the great Kratch to rip this Tooth from his side?"

The General lied saying that Kratch didn't even flinch.

Megadon and Naw withdrew to inspect the note.

"'Megadon,

'It appears we must meet again, my old nemesis, if you want to save this creature of light you call the Millennium Angel. General Slash has informed you of her recent capture and imprisonment in an impenetrable cave of coral. In the Map of Currents before you, you will find a series of territories you must pass through at various times.

'You can find me in all of these places at any time.

'Consequently, your chances to eliminate me will be many. Your warriors must follow the map as it is laid out.

'First, they must pass through the Burrows of the Giant Worms, then pass Canyons of Perpetual Darkness and finally, past the home of Tentacle the Giant Squid.

'If you succeed, and have yet to find me, then I will surely find you in this final place on the map.

'You know this place. It is where men kill the whales. The Tooth you see is essential in order to eliminate me. Your warriors will need keener judgment of where to place this Tooth than you had if they intend to mortally wound me. Perhaps they will avenge your wife for you.'"

At this reference, Megadon showed a rare look of rage. He returned to reading the note:

"'The key to freeing the Angel is eliminating me.

'If you win, I will relinquish my world of evil to you and will be gone from the planet forever.

'If you lose, I will take your kingdom, and you will be banished from earth for all time.

'When I have been defeated, the Jellyfish Wizard will disenchant the cave and free the Angel. I await your reply!

Lord of Darkness

Kratch'"

Megadon and Naw went to the surface to seek a sign from the All Knowing. A new day was dawning as the ocean came to life. Light scattered upon the surface like raindrop jewels fallen from the sky. A bright yellow cloud mass illuminated the sky. And a Voice came from the clouds as Megadon and Naw watched intently. A soft deep voice spoke to the two troubled leaders.

"Megadon, my Son of the Light," said the All Knowing, it will be a difficult task for you to win this challenge. Your son, Naw, must be the judge of whether he will risk his life to save the Millennium Angel. I will not challenge your decisions. Do you understand?"

Megadon made it clear that he understood.

The All Knowing swirled the ball of light around Naw and Megadon filling them with love and hope. In a moment, the All Knowing vanished into nothingness.

Megadon opened the Map of Currents and he inspected the route laid out by Kratch.

"Naw," began Megadon. "This is a trap. These currents are steady and strong and even the best of swimmers could be swept into danger. I do not like it."

Naw jumped in with his own thoughts. "If no one accepts this evil challenge then the Millennium Angel will perish and her light will be lost. We cannot afford to be weak here father, I accept the challenge and the consequences."

"Let's think it over tonight and if you feel the same in the morning, then so be it," Megadon responded.

Before the morning light, Naw appeared at Megadon's bedside unexpectedly to say goodbye to his father. Only one soldier accompanied him.

"Father, I have decided to take leave this morning for the Canyons of Perpetual Darkness. My friend, Snap, is going with me. He is, I'm sorry to say, the only volunteer."

"Wait Naw!" Megadon said angrily. "I will command many others to go with you,"

"No, I don't wish to take any that don't believe in the success of this mission, and most don't. I have the Map, the

Tooth, my friend Snap and my courage. That will be enough. Goodbye father."

Megadon was stunned. "The All Knowing will be with you, and so will I. Please be careful, and be wise in your choices of action against Kratch, my son. Goodbye."

A dark cloud of foreboding settled over Megadon as he watched his son and his lone companion swim away.

Sunrise came quickly for the two confident Great White Sharks. They entered the first of the challenges, the Burrows of the Giant Worms. The day was so bright that rays of sun penetrated all the way to the bottom exposing a soft sandy bottom. Naw was looking for signs of the deadly Worms. Not a single form of life moved with the exception of plants drifting in the current.

Naw and Snap made it through the Burrows by sunset that day without incident. To Naw, this was simply a blessing from the All Knowing. The next morning they would enter the Canyons of Perpetual Darkness.

"Surely the All Knowing would work the same magic for them," Naw declared.

Naw and Snap came to the second obstacle in the Map of Currents. They slowly began their descent into this pitch dark blue water.

Naw nudged Snap. "Look Snap, isn't that a source of light ahead?"

They both looked to see a clear path of light that formed a tunnel. It was hypnotizing and Naw thought it was a sign from the All Knowing. They swam into the orange and yellow glow, watching as the Canyons lighted up before them. As they continued, the light became so bright that they were blinded. Naw and Snap stopped, but before they could react, the Bullycudas were upon them.

The light was an illusion created by the Jellyfish Wizard. He joined the Bullycudas and wrapped his tentacles around Naw and wrestled the Tooth from him. The Wizard then turned his attention to Snap and dragged him away from the capture of Naw.

The Jellyfish Wizard locked his gaze into Snap's horrified eyes. Snap froze with fear. The Jellyfish Wizard let the Tooth drop as Snap looked on in disbelief.

"Go and tell Megadon of the capture of his son. He will be taken to Kratch and held prisoner. Do you understand?"

Snap nodded and quickly fled the scene. Snap knew he had to get help and he left with the Map still tucked under his flipper. He also knew where the Tooth had been dropped and he could return another day and retrieve it.

Snap returned to Megadon with news of the ambush and the unusual role of the Jellyfish Wizard. He told Megadon that Kratch was nowhere to be seen and that the Wizard had dropped the Tooth and allowed him to escape with the map.

Megadon pondered this information. "That doesn't make sense. Snap," he said.

"I know," replied Snap.

Megadon brightened for a moment, saying, "We have

the map, and the Tooth can surely be found, so there is still hope."

Megadon sent Snap to find volunteers that would attempt the rescue of Naw and undertake the completion of his mission. Snap returned to tell Megadon that none of his soldiers were willing to face Kratch or the Jellyfish Wizard without their leader Megadon.

Megadon shook his head in disgust and told Snap that there were good reasons why he could not be part of the rescue. "Snap. we must rely on the All Knowing for our solution."

The evening skies were especially dark this night as Snap and Megadon swam past the soldiers on their way to rest. The soldiers turned away from the harsh and judging eyes of their leader.

Megadon's normally restful sleep was filled with visions of his captured son. During one dream Megadon awoke abruptly. He thought he had heard the voice of the All Knowing. The voice said, "Be patient. The Light of our world is always at work for you Megadon. The Worthy One's are on the way."

Megadon repeated these words in a whisper and soon fell into a healing sleep.

The fate of the oceans was held in the balance, and the lives of Naw and the Millennium Angel were in peril.

Chapter Two

OFF TO STUDY THE WHALES

Deep pockets of cobalt blue speckled the nutrient rich green waters of the narrow harbor as the motor vessel *Krill* eased into a sandbar riddled channel that led to the dock. Countless bird species played out their daily feeding rituals in the shallow tide pools as two lovers walked through ankle deep water, hands locked, oblivious to the Great Blue Herons flying overhead. The herons descended noiselessly, landing behind the lovers, and prepared to feast in the shallows of the exposed beach.

Young Ned Miller continued to clean the *Krill* as the vessel moved through the channel. The *Krill* was a vintage forty-two foot Chris Craft, with wooden decks, rails of brass, and a variety of nautical accessories adorning her cockpit and cabin. The students who studied with professors Miller, Conway and Blanchard took great pride in keeping her in top condition. Maintenance was the professor's top priority. The sides were painted a brilliant white and her bottom a deep blue with a red stripe at the waterline. The decks were covered with layers of clear shellac that sparkled in the sun. The old boat was a veteran of many voyages, and the coming three weeks the *Krill* and its crew would see an attempt to follow the humpback's southern migration.

Professor Miller's research vessel *Krill* passed the Number Four Buoy. They had completed a successful day of research and spent the afternoon studying a dozen whales. The professors were comparing their notes in the pilothouse, but couldn't help an occasional look away from each other to drink in the beauty of the surrounding harbor.

The peaceful ambience of the moment was shattered by the sounds of pans and glass hitting the deck of the galley floor below. Professor Conway moved toward the cabin to check on Ned but was quickly restrained by the boy's father. Miller assured him that his son was nothing more than a clumsy kid who could clean up his own mess. If Ned were hurt he would call for help. Conway reluctantly accepted Miller's harsh assessment and remained with the two professors. In the uneasy silence that befell the trio, Ned's father reluctantly called down to the galley to check on the boy.

"I'm fine," Ned replied flatly.

As Ned turned back to the mess in the galley, he caught a glimpse of his teary eyes in the mirror attached to the bathroom door. He paused for a moment and examined his thin frame and the long arms devoid of muscle tone. His pock marked face was reddened by the wind and his hair a dirty blond mop forever flopping in his face. Ned saw a homely boy in the glass. Often he became the target of taunts and teasing from others.

As the boat neared the final buoys marking the tricky

channel, the *Krill*'s captain spied the dock. Ned came up from the galley and began to curl the lines on the starboard side. Approaching the dock were five of Miller's students, one prepared to catch the lines as the vessel neared the first row of aged pilings at the dock

Old tires draped wooden pilings as gulls perched atop tar streaked helmets of metal covering the top of these sentries. Sailors busied themselves with presail duties.

Ned tossed the first line overboard, hitting the water and missing the dock by a few inches. The outstretched arm of the student on the dock couldn't compensate for the poor toss.

"You're a klutz, Ned. Throw it right next time!"

By now, the *Krill* was close enough to the dock to simply drop the line to the outstretched hand of a student who said sarcastically to Ned: "Thanks sailor."

Ned retreated to the stern with his head hanging and tossed the stern line to waiting hands.

Professor Blanchard waddled his way to the bow squeezing between the rail and the life buoys that lined the cabin's exterior. Blanchard was short, balding, wore thick glasses, and was at least 60 pounds overweight. His sleeveless T-shirt only accentuated the rolls of fat on his upper body. He coiled the bowline and tossed it perfectly onto the dock as the boat was now secured.

"It's all in the toss," Blanchard told Ned. Ned retreated to the galley.

Professor Conway was smaller than Blanchard and had

a kindly look about him. He went into the galley and bent down to help Ned pick up a final pieces of glass. He could see that Ned had been crying and reached over to tickle him in the ribs. "Don't listen to that Blanchard, Ned," he whispered. "He may know whales, but he's a fool when it comes to people."

Ned smiled and wiped his eyes. "Thanks Professor Conway."

As Conway picked up the last piece of glass, he said to Ned, "You're going to be someone very special someday, and your father's going to see what a great son he has."

Professor Blanchard joined the group of students and found them engaged with Professor Miller who was relating the highlights of their day offshore with the whales. Miller's salt and pepper hair blew gently over his sunburned forehead exposing a deep receding hairline. A portly belly protruded ever so slightly over his sea knot designer belt, the only flaw in an otherwise thin frame. His nose was a sore point with him as he had received his mother's finer features and his father's toucan-like nose. He wore khaki shorts with ankle socks, and whale-embroidered polo shirt that represented the uniform for the crew. The chest pockets revealed the nickname of the boat, "*The Krill Craft*" and an embroidered whale.

The activity on the *Krill* accelerated as the students swarmed over the decks to place the supplies they would need during the trip. Sandpaper and gallons of shellac and paint were delivered aboard, much to the dismay of the students. Past experience had shown that they would be using every drop of paint and every sheet of sandpaper.

Ned had many unhappy memories of the years as a cabin boy in the *Krill*. He had cleaned the decks of the seasick and occasionally drunken students. Now fourteen, he realized he had become a slave to his father during these voyages. He hated the trips with a passion. He had to be awake before anyone else, and was the last to sleep until all the daily work was done. He became a decent cook and had learned a great deal about whales, although he rarely had the chance to share his talent or knowledge with anyone. He seldom spoke to anyone nor was he spoken to, so, his opinion became his lone roommate, a companion to his low self esteem. In his isolation and unhappiness he realized that no one noticed and no one seemed to care about him.

The professor called the students to the galley area to review the charts showing where the whales would be found during their 1500 mile journey. The charts were carefully placed in succession to reflect the progress they would make during the trip. Ned listened to his father's talk of underwater mountain ranges, encounters with sharks and rare birds, and the search for whales that would consume them in the weeks ahead.

"We will be tracking the sounds of whales that echo off the high bottom so we can learn more about how the whales navigate during their migration. I plan to prove that sound is, in fact, how the whales navigate the world over," the professor pontificated. "We will gather all the sound data at the end of the journey, and this winter we will analyze our findings and hopefully prove our theory."

Holding up a large chart he went on. "Here are the lookout schedules, and I will not tolerate sleeping, drinking, or goofing off while on duty. Do you all understand?" he asked.

The students looked at the professor and nodded. Then he asked them to gather at the chart table and familiarize themselves with the maps of the ocean floor. He reminded them that Ned was on board to assist them at any time.

"Try to excuse the boy's clumsy ways," he apologized. "I think he must have the mailman's genes. I can't imagine that anyone so quiet and clumsy could be my son."

Ned, who was still listening intently, lowered his head and slipped back into his room, closing and locking the door. That evening Ned had the strangest dreams of an odd colored bird and a sparkling blue eyed dolphin.

The crew of the *Krill* awakened as the sunrise crept over the tranquil harbor. The boat's portholes were illuminated by the suns rays, alerting the well rested students, Ned, and the professor that it was time to get up. Ned peeked through his window at the westerly portion of the bay. Spatina grass flowed in a hypnotic dance over the acres of salt marsh as the wind choreographed the morning ballet of sea grass. Wisps of salt streaked over the glass of Ned's window to splinter the sea and sand in a kaleidoscope of fragmented oceanscapes.

The water's surface sparkled across the harbor's calm waters. A handful of terns and gulls accented this natural alarm clock of sunshine with their peeps and caws. Sun and sound became the wake up call from Earth, beckoning them to begin their adventure.

Ned brewed a pot of coffee and poured the pancakes on the grill in preparation of the morning meal. Ned's father arrived in the galley of the boat helping himself to Ned's coffee. He moved Ned aside to get a spoon and nodded a morning greeting to his son, patting Ned on the head. This token was the extent of the thanks and affection ever shown to him. It was all Ned's father could muster. Ned, of course, was willing to accept any gesture over none at all.

"Good morning Dad," Ned said to the retreating back.

Next, the students piled into the galley to gulp down coffee and pour gobs of syrup over the delightful pancakes Ned had prepared for them. The meal soon ended as the motors thrummed and the crew began the familiar routine of departure.

As the end of the channel came into view, the *Krill's* wake churned heartily giving the last red channel buoy a lingering sway to the right and left as she passed. Now in the open ocean, the *Krill* would begin her journey.

Within twenty hours the first group of whales were sighted and the crew eagerly began collecting data. Hydrophones were slipped over the stern and the students were poised over their clipboards in readiness for the first sign of significant data. The technicians wore headphones and were responsible for the recording of the myriad of jumbled sounds of the sea. To them, the noises were the ocean's symphony.

A humpback cow and her calf leaped one hundred yards from the stern and the students doffed their headphones. The deafening sound of whales hitting the water was likened to an explosion to those listening on the hydrophones. The stout bodies of two more whales joined the cow and calf as they began to blow massive walls of neon bubbles underwater to confuse and corral nearby schools of fish. This was a technique that the *Krill*'s crew had witnessed many times. The giant open mouth of the first humpback came to the surface through the bubbles, small fish leaking, and flying over the sides of its gaping mouth. The whale snapped its jaws closed, trapping over a hundred pounds of fish in a moment. The feeding scene played itself out over and over as the day slipped onward.

The high point of the day was the successful darting of one of the larger whales with a radio tag. Already it had produced a traceable signal, which the crew could use to map the whale's southerly voyage. That day the *Krill* sighted a total of seventy whales.

Everyone hoped that these whales were now beginning their migration south and that the *Krill* would be able to follow them. Ned announced dinner as the crew gathered to consume a hearty meal of spaghetti and garlic bread. In the festive atmosphere of the opening night, Professor Miller regaled them with his favorite "whale tale."

Lubricated by a few glasses of wine, the professor once again told of his best day aboard the *Krill*. "My students of ten years ago," he began, standing at the head of the table and peering down as his dutiful students sat listening, "had the good fortune of being aboard the *Krill*, when we found ourselves magically trapped by over one hundred whales. In the outer circle there were Right Whales. On the inside there were thirty to forty humpbacks, and another thirty finbacks and fifty pilot whales. For as far as the eye could see, there were hundreds of white sided dolphins mixing in and out of a feeding frenzy that was no less than a square mile of ocean," the professor boasted. "One could have stepped off the boat and walked on the backs of the whales, there were so many.

"To top it off, massive schools of thousand pound tuna joined the melee, as whales, dolphins, and tuna competed for acres of fish. This school of fish packed the waters to 300 feet. We simply shut down the engines and watched this most spectacular display of nature at her finest."

As always he ended his story with the well known last line: "They could have buried me that day. It was the happiest moment of my life."

The students clapped obligingly, as they always did.

The festivities were suddenly cut short as Ned alerted his father to the odor of an engine overheating. Professor Miller rushed to the engine room and immediately shut down the port engine. A brief inspection of the problem disclosed a burst hose. Oil levels had reached a dangerously low level and Ned's quick response had most likely saved the engine. His father was looking for oil to replace the lost fluid when Ned realized he had forgotten the three five gallon containers the professors had purchased at the marina. With all his other responsibilities, he had overlooked the need for extra oil.

His father was livid and berated him in his fury so that all the crew could hear every demeaning and humiliating remark. Ned had managed to ruin the trip. Without that oil they would need to find a port immediately with only one working engine. This effectively destroyed any chance they had of following the darted whale.

"The mission is ruined," Miller bellowed. "The next port is 150 miles away going six knots an hour." This news drew a heavy sigh of defeat from the students.

The verbal assault on Ned ended in front of the students as the professor told his son he wished he had never been born! Ned couldn't listen to anymore and ran to his bunk to hide.

Hundreds of miles away a strong set of weather systems took an unexpected turn toward the coast and the *Krill* as she set her course for port. If these systems converged and joined forces they contained an immense potential threat for mariners and coastal residents alike.

TV weatherman Al Gilman, was just beginning to see the latest computer images of the storm making way to land. He scurried to his manager's office to request permission to issue a storm advisory.

Professor Miller was soon on the cell phone to Professors Blanchard and Conway asking their help in procuring oil and other parts needed by the *Krill*. The two professors had never made the journey south on the *Krill*, as the college's fall semester was in session during the whale migration. The university wouldn't allow leave for all three professors. They assured Miller that the needed supplies would be there when *Krill* reached port. Miller hung up feeling relieved that he had two such loyal friends and associates.

In the distance, sounds of rumbling thunder cascaded from the horizon and the clouds were streaked coal black.

Blanchard and Conway were calling the marina's to arrange for supplies when a student rushed in to tell them of the latest weather advisory. The two professors switched to TV channel seven for the full details. There they caught the report from weatherman Al Gilman.

"We repeat," the concerned meteorologist was saying. "The two systems now colliding off to our east and north have begun to create sustained winds of sixty to eighty miles per hour. Seas of ten to thirty feet can be expected! Any persons on the water should get to port immediately."

Professor Conway's face creased with worry as he ran to his cell phone to call the *Krill*. The phone rang many times until the operator informed him that all the circuits were temporarily out and that line crews were repairing them as rapidly as possible. She apologized for any inconvenience. Conway looked desperately at Blanchard and shook his head in despair. Conway broke the awkward silence and told Blanchard he would attempt to call every fifteen minutes.

Meanwhile, the *Krill* was making good time as tide and current worked to accelerate her journey inland. The crew reported that they were now fifty miles from port and that perhaps another call to Conway would be helpful in expediting the delivery of supplies. Miller calculated they could salvage the trip south if they could leave port in one day.

Gusts of wind began to sweep the surface of the ocean and white caps curled the wave crests. The *Krill*'s radio reception was poor since they were so far from shore, while the rapid development of foul weather surprised the professor and his crew.

The VHF radio was being worked on by one of the students, and a faint and scratchy voice faded in and out of the tiny speaker mounted alongside it. The boy, who had adjusted the radio sat with his ear pressed to the speaker. His youthful face paled to ash as he began to relate the tattered details from the weather service. "Winds of sixty to eighty MPH and ten to thirty foot seas in the next five to ten hours," he repeated.

The professor's expression was grim as he looked out the cabin window, noticing the seas were already at least six feet high. But this was no time for him to show fear. He swung into action issuing orders to his crew. The lab equipment and all their gear were to be lashed down and secured below decks.

Ned came in and asked what he could do to help.

"Just stay out of the way!" his father snapped.

Ned knew his father would hold this grudge for the entire trip. The thought of three weeks of such emotional pain was unfathomable. His eyes began to fill with tears and his chin trembled uncontrollably. He quickly left the frenzy of activity in the pilothouse and headed for the stern.

Despair filled the lad as he folded his arms and laid his tear soaked eyes over them. His muffled cries were drowned out by the sounds of the rising storm. He began the lonely walk back to his cabin but was suddenly knocked off of his feet as a freak wave hit the *Krill* broadside. Ned grabbed hopelessly at the polished brass rail at the stern. With one hand wrapped tightly to the boat's rail, Ned screamed wildly for help. The powerful howling of the wind blew his cries away. His fingers lost their grip and within seconds another wave struck and sent Ned overboard. His arms were flailing and his desperate cries for help went unheard. The boat was rocking wildly from port to starboard and its crew held on for dear life.

Ned bobbed in the heavy surf remembering his father's last wish that he had never been born. Ned thought he had seen his father looking back at him as he held on to the rail of the *Krill*. In his turmoil, he believed that his father had ignored his dilemma and decided to keep going. Ned tumbled in the curling seas of green white foam and rolled helplessly under the dark and cold water.

Thoughts of his father were now replaced by the knowledge that his end was near. He was drowning as he swallowed gulp after gulp of salty water.

Conway was making his tenth attempt to contact the *Krill* when he finally got through. The relieved professor spilled out the weather details and Miller assured Conway that he was already plowing the *Krill* through the outer edge of the storm.

"The worst of it is still developing," informed Conway.

"Yes, I know," replied Miller. "Luckily we're only thirty miles out now and are able to receive the marine weather."

"It's a good thing Ned forgot the oil, or you'd still be a hundred and fifty miles offshore and undoubtedly you'd all be dead," stated Conway.

After a few seconds of silence, Miller sighed. "Yes, I suppose that's true, Conway," he responded. "It appears my son has unwittingly saved our lives."

"I'm sure he would appreciate hearing that," suggested Conway. "You know you're very hard on that boy."

"The minute we hit port, I'm going to give Ned the biggest hug he's ever had," promised Miller. "I'm going to let him know how much I love him."

The phone went dead as contact was again severed by heavy winds.

One of the research students returned to the pilothouse of the *Krill* to report on the condition of the boat in general. The young man entered the cabin hurriedly and was breathing heavily.

"What is going on?" queried Professor Miller.

"It's Ned, sir," said the panicked student. "He's not on board."

"Have you checked everywhere?" the professor insisted, a father's worst fear rising in him.

"Yes, we've all looked all over, and he's vanished," the student said, starting to sob.

Professor Miller leapt to the VHF radio, fumbling for the mic. "Coast Guard, Coast Guard," he called frantically. "This is the motor vessel *Krill*. Mayday, Mayday! Man overboard!"

He hesitated a moment, then whispered into the mic, "My son is gone overboard. I've lost my precious son."

The professor repeated the call again before the Coast Guard responded with instructions to the *Krill* that her crew comes to port immediately and not to attempt a search or rescue in these horrific conditions. The professor slumped in his chair as he realized that Ned was most likely in the hands of God. In a rare display of emotion he held his head in his hands and shuddered as his body racked with sobs. A crewman assumed the helm as the professor left the pilothouse to stare at the churning sea.

Chapter Three

THE OCEAN HAVEN

The unruly sea consumed Ned's strength. Amidst his continual struggle, he noticed a colorful bird flying in circles above him. It's beautiful beak was a pumpkin orange and a golden yellow band encircled its mid section and tail. The wings were pitch black edged with a brilliant blue green color. Ned had certainly never seen a bird like this one before. He was fixated on the spiraling visitor as he was tossed about in the heavy seas. The more the bird made circles overhead the dizzier Ned became!

Ned looked away to see a dorsal fin break the choppy horizon. Fear and desperation filled his every fiber as the dorsal and body of a dolphin came to the surface right next to him. He reached for the dorsal as if it was intentionally offered and he held on. The dolphin obliged Ned with a ride through the waves as the colorful bird flew overhead following them. The bird flew directly at Ned and he was pelted with a series of heavy oily drops coming from under the bird's wings.

The dolphin continued to pull Ned through the seas. He suddenly felt very tired, then dizzy just as the dolphin made a sharp downward arch taking Ned deep. Ned saw nothing but water before he passed out.

Unaware of his fate, Ned rested on a moss filled ledge in the depths of the ocean. His dreams were filled with episodes of sea creatures rubbing against his legs and of an octopus straddling his head and inspecting him closely. Ned awoke with a start to find himself deep in the ocean. He was alive. He seemed somewhat sure of that.

He felt his body all over to assure himself his assumption was correct. "Am I in heaven?" He wondered. He examined the mossy ledge where he had rested and awoke to find a shell with a purplish fluid dissolving and rising into the water. Picking up this shell he remembered it as one of the objects in his early dreams of this mysterious place.

Looking around, Ned could see the bubbles of his breathing rising toward the surface. Further investigation revealed six bulging eyes staring at him from a ledge less than one hundred feet away. A shiver of fear paralyzed him. Whatever was staring back at him could be sizing him up for its next meal.

As he was deciding what to do next, the long bottled snout of a dolphin began to curl around the ledge. The dolphin swam to Ned in seconds that seemed an eternity to the terrified boy.

He recognized this dolphin as the one that accompanied him in his deep plunge to this strange new water world. She had large blue eyes that emitted streams of white light, and had an aura of peace about them. This immediately put Ned into a gentle state of relaxation. The graceful, deliberate and slow undulations of this beautiful dolphin had Ned mesmerized.

Inspecting him, she moved closer. Ned was sure he could detect a shy smile from this enticing mammal of the deep. The dolphin suddenly made a powerful sweep of her body accelerating past her unsuspecting onlooker with blinding speed. Ned quickly looked around to try and relocate this most delightful creature. He found her instead by the sound of a giggle coming from directly behind him.

He turned about to see the dolphin smiling inches from him. She began to speak to Ned, her eyes fixed on his. Ned felt a strange new sensation all over his body as he realized he was falling in love. He blushed and his body went limp at the sight of her eyes. They were sparkling pools of blue joy.

Pushing the shell next to Ned with her snout she looked at Ned. "I see the Ocean Potion has worked nicely for you. She paused awkwardly. "Who are you?"

"My name is Ned. Who are you?"

"I am Eccoh," the dolphin giggled. "The other eyes staring at you are my friends, Kila and Flop." Eccoh beckoned to the two whales. "Come over here you two and meet Ned. After all, he was sent to us by Dawinn."

Ned wondered who Dawinn was. The first to leave the ledge was a humpback whale that edged around the great rock followed by a nervous killer whale. The killer whale's dorsal was bent to one side.

"Who did you say sent me here?" Ned asked Eccoh.

"Ned," Eccoh began. "Dawinn is our connection to the light of the world. He forewarned us you would need our help, and for some reason we would need yours." She finished as Flop approached.

"Pleased to meet you, Ned," Flop said, extending his long white flipper over Ned's back, offering him a welcome pat.

"Why, it's very nice to meet you too, Flop," Ned responded politely.

Kila still floated next to the ledge as Eccoh managed to sneak up behind Kila without him noticing. She bumped him from behind and scared him right in the direction of Ned.

Kila let out a high pitched squeal after bumping Ned and knocking him right into Flop. The three of them rolled on the sandy bottom stirring up the sand. Eccoh and Flop laughed at Ned and Kila as they composed themselves.

"Thank you, thank you very much," Kila squirted out while moving a safe distance from Ned.

Flop jumped in explaining to Ned about Kila. "Poor Kila is afraid of everything in the ocean, Ned, and the way you came here had Kila convinced that you are an ally of the evil Kratch."

Ned thought about this for a moment. "I wonder who Kratch is?" he said to himself.

Now it was Kila's turn to expose Flop's shortcomings. "Oh, Flop loves to tell you all about my fears, but he can't even breach. What do you think about that, Ned?"

Eccoh interrupted them and insisted on quiet, but Ned's curiosity was so overpowering, he asked the whales to please tell him why he was there and how he got there?

Eccoh came forward to within a foot of Ned. "Ned, when you were in that awful storm, the bird we call Dawinn sprinkled a potion over you that has given you this life underwater. We call this place the Ocean Haven because we have all been deemed unworthy. In order to live with the other whales of the world we are forced to stay in a very confined area. Of course, we could leave, but we would most likely be taken by sharks or who knows what. Here we are given protection and assurance of a safe life together. So it is here we stay."

Ned interrupted Eccoh. "What do you mean you are deemed unworthy?"

"We cannot perform as other whales do," Eccoh explained. "Flop can't breach, and so cannot communicate with other whales easily. Kila is afraid of everything. I cannot echolocate and can't hear the other dolphins. I can't stun food to catch it. Do you understand?" Eccoh asked softly.

Before Ned could answer, the nervous Kila felt compelled to add his share of the tale. "You see Ned, we are forced to live in this specific territory which happens to be surrounded by sharks, all of whom would love to have us for a meal. Luckily, they don't bother us, thanks to Megadon."

"Who is Megadon?" Ned asked.

"Well now," Flop answered. "Megadon is the keeper of balance and light in the oceans. He allows us to inhabit this protected area. It has been designated as the Ocean Haven, and we can live here under one condition. That is, that all whales who perish because of old age, or for any reason, allow their bodies to be delivered to Megadon and his soldiers to eat.

"So," Flop went on, "when a whale leaves his physical body and heads to the light, the body is of no use except as a meal to sharks. This offering is of no harm to us since the soul of our brothers and sisters have been delivered to the All Knowing.

"So, in serving the shark's hunger, Megadon's soldiers don't bother us. But, if we stray from the boundaries of the Ocean Haven, we are subject to the laws of the great ocean, which is simply: Eat or be Eaten"

Eccoh interrupted the talkative and philosophic Flop. "There is a great Blue Whale that has grown old and died, choosing to leave this world and go into the light. He will be delivered to the sharks at the next dawn of light. Would you like to see him, Ned?" she asked.

"Oh my! Could I?" Ned asked.

"What if the sharks are already there and we get eaten?" worried Kila.

"We have nothing to fear," Eccoh said. "Megadon is expecting the Blue Whale and will restrain his soldiers until the new day is here. But before we swim anywhere Ned, you must drink the remaining Ocean Potion, which will complete your adaptation to underwater life. The transformation will be quite uncomfortable for you," she explained. "We were told to wait until you seemed comfortable with us before offering it to you."

There on the ledge was a shell containing the Ocean Potion. "You must drink this, Ned, if you wish to stay here. The choice is yours."

Ned didn't hesitate as he grasped the shell and quickly drank the purple potion. Kila and Flop moved back and Eccoh moved to Ned's side to support him.

For long moments nothing happened and then suddenly he began experiencing waves of pain that shook him to the core. He writhed in agony as Eccoh floated helplessly by his side. Soon his hands and feet began to grow into webs and flippers. On his back, rippling new muscle formed. His legs merged and his feet became a tail.

As the pain subsided, Ned realized that he had become a sleek young dolphin. He felt like he could fly through the water. A dolphin's body replaced the boy that he had been, while the only reminder if his humanness was in his eyes and the sandy hair that flopped over the side of his new snout and melon.

Eccoh swam over and gently kissed Ned on his new dolphin cheek. Kila and Flop began to make sounds of delight in the form of clicks, whistles and high pitched squeals. Ned was now truly one of them.

Quickly, they made their way into the open waters to follow Eccoh to the resting place of the Blue Whale. Kila stayed directly behind Eccoh and Flop. The three whales carved a path through the crystal clear waters and led Ned to the Blue Whale.

On the way to the Blue Whale, Ned was spellbound by the colors of the many small schooling fish that passed fearlessly by the moving foursome. He was astounded and captivated by this splendid new universe.

It seemed like only seconds later that the massive whale came into view. The Blue Whale seemed alive as this gargantuan creature was undulating with the current. Light patterns glowed endless geometric shapes over the body, while the current moved the soft rubbery flesh of the tail and flippers just enough to give it the appearance of life.

Ned stopped and marveled at this incredulous sight as the others made a three hundred and sixty degree pass around the whale. Ned floated motionless by the eye of the whale which was wide open. The eye became a mirror to Ned who could now see and appreciate the new form the Ocean Potion had given him. There was softness to the whale's eye; serenity — a sensation Ned had never felt. It was as if the Blue Whale stared into the boy's soul and Ned could feel tears push from his eyes and disappear into the vastness of salty water. The combination of his new being and the remembrance of the pitiful boy he had been was a cocktail for more tears. Ned wept openly, and absorbed something magical into his being before breaking free of the spell the eye had on him.

Ned composed himself and laid his flipper-like hand

over the eye of the Blue Whale. That huge eye stared back at Ned seeming to beg Ned to close it for him, a final gesture before his eternal rest.

Ned held his flipper there for a moment and said a prayer for this most elegant sleeping giant.

It was time to find his comrades now and Ned looked down the length of the massive whale. He began to make out the tail of Flop who was propelling himself around the twenty-foot flukes of the Blue. Kila followed Flop and Eccoh followed Kila during a game of chase that became a kaleidoscope of florescent bodies changing shape and color to the point where they meshed as one animal, spinning around the massive tail of the Blue Whale. Ned was now a world of game's and wonderment that he embraced easily.

That desperation of never belonging had suddenly taken a ghost-like exodus from his body. At that moment, the three whales stopped playing only long enough to invite Ned in the game of chase. The games only reward being a love and dedication to one another's well being.

When the fun ended, the four misfits of the marine mammal world rested atop the Blue Whale. Eccoh and Ned each were stretched out in one of the flesh like hammocks that the blowholes formed. Flop and Kila opted for the curvature of the tail as they were rocked slowly up and down into a deep sleep. The gentle whoosh of water below the tail was all the white noise they needed to keep the magnitude of ocean sounds from interrupting the dreams of these worn out whales.

Eccoh was the first one to wake and she nudged Ned to wake him. Eccoh seemed disturbed and swam away from Ned's questioning look. Kila and Flop were slow to awake from their tremulous dreams. Eccoh suddenly shoved Kila, scaring him off the tail and onto the sandy bottom. Flop was next and he, too, rolled into the sand.

"What was that all about, Eccoh?" insisted Flop.

Eccoh swam in circles as if pondering a big problem. "I've been thinking that I want to leave the Ocean Haven and live as the others do," she stated.

Kila laughed and replied, "Oh sure Eccoh, what are you going to do to protect yourself or survive?"

Flop didn't miss his chance to question Eccoh 's thinking. "Eccoh, we have all talked about this before, and you know I can't breach. Therefore, I can't stun fish for food or communicate. So if I get lost, I'm as good as gone. And what about Kila? He wouldn't last a day! And you, Eccoh, would never be able to communicate with the other dolphins and be an outcast without a home. At least we have each other and a safe place to live. Stop this lunacy!"

Even Ned could see that none of them would survive in this unforgiving environment. Eccoh began to cry. Ned extended his flippers to hug her, but she jolted herself loose. Eccoh then made violent gestures as she darted at great speeds right at the Blue as if she were going to crash into the side of the lifeless whale's ribs. Kila and Flop were horrified at her behavior, something they had never seen from Eccoh.

Finally she slowed down and hovered over the dorsal fin of the Blue Whale. Drifting toward the head, she turned to see her concerned friends move toward her in unison. She was upset, and Ned spoke to her as they gathered around the mammoth head of the dead Blue Whale.

A silence fell over the group, and no one looked at one another until Eccoh began to let out her thoughts to them. "I'm sorry for being so crazy," she announced. "But I'm telling you now that I intend to leave this place even if it means I'm going to die. I can't go through life without feeling some purpose to it other than relying on the other fit whales to care for us!

"Tomorrow morning I plan to swim past the safe territory of the Ocean Haven and find some other dolphins."

The group was speechless. Flop asked Eccoh to please reconsider and give the notion until the new moon to reflect on the wisdom of her choice. Eccoh just swam aimlessly out of sight. Before she disappeared she stopped and turned to them. "I'll miss you." she said, and swam away.

Ned shouted across the head of the Blue Whale for her to halt. He said he had a purpose for them all if she'd listen. She came back, her eyes were a curious mix of excitement and fear all in one. Ned claimed he was about to introduce them to the challenge of a lifetime!

Gathering along the jaws of the Blue Whale they were instructed to sit and listen to what he had to tell them. Kila rolled his eyes back dreading any possible scheme that would take him from this safe haven he had called home for his entire life.

Ned proceeded to tell them about whaling, and the horrors that the fittest of the whales had to endure. The misfit's eyes bulged wide with fascination as Ned wove his tale. Ned proposed that maybe they could all escape the Ocean Haven, and together they could stop this heinous crime.

The big question was how?

Eccoh was the first to speak. She told Ned that even without a plan that they would formulate one on the way to the whaling grounds. This was certainly more acceptable than staying at the Ocean Haven feeling useless.

Ned and Flop also agreed and they all looked to Kila, huddled under the lip of the Blue Whale and shivering uncontrollably. Flop and Ned lifted the heavy upper jaw of the Blue Whale to get to Kila. He did not want to leave, telling them straight out he would not go with them. "How. are you going to get past the sharks tomorrow morning?" Kila asked Ned.

"Flop," Ned asked. "Do these sharks all gather at the outer edges of the Ocean Haven and eat as much of this Blue Whale as they can the first day? And, can these sharks consume this big a whale in one day?"

"No, Ned, it takes weeks before they actually get to the bones and the final bites from a whale this great," Flop told Ned. "After each day they all rest together with Megadon.

The great leader used to fill the nights with tales of his heroics against Kratch, the Lord of Darkness."

"Why do you say 'used to' tell tales?" asked Ned.

Eccoh piped in and insisted Ned tell of how he planned to escape the Ocean Haven before they fill the time with stories of the great and magnificent Megadon. Ned put his flipper under his chin.

"I know how we can get out," Ned commanded like a true leader. "You told me that others will drag this Blue Whale to the sharks, and the sharks normally take weeks to devour it all, right?"

They all nodded agreement except Kila, who was nervous seeing the group was intrigued with Ned's plan.

Ned went on. "At first light we will all get inside the mouth of the Blue Whale and close it tight. Then when the escorts arrive to drag it to the sharks we will be secretly delivered to freedom from this place. Once the sharks stop feeding that first day we will then open the mouth while they rest and swim away. While they are spending time with this Megadon character we will make our escape."

"Simply wonderful!" Flop exclaimed.

"I love it," Eccoh agreed.

They all turned to Kila who had already begun to swim to the ledge where the adventure had begun for Ned. Flop began to swim after him, but the strong willed Eccoh stopped him. Flop and Eccoh realized that unless Kila changed his mind, it would be the last they ever saw of their life long pal. It was a painful moment for them.

"If we don't do something now we will surely have spent our lives as nothing but worthless souls in the grand scheme of things," Eccoh said.

It was all that she needed to say. Flop, who loved Kila more than any of them, realized she was right. Ned spoke up to break the cable of pain in the eye's of Eccoh and Flop who followed Kila's every inch of departure. Ned asked Flop about Megadon. Reluctantly Flop broke his gaze of Kila.

Eccoh and Ned nestled inside the rubbery confines of the blowhole while Flop stretched out next to them to tell Ned of Megadon and the tragic loss of his beloved son, Naw. The story ended with the description of the Map of Currents, the lost Tooth, the Jellyfish Wizard and finally, of the Millennium Angel.

All this made for a most fascinating tale. Ned told his new friends what an honor it would be to help someone like Megadon. Flop and Eccoh only laughed at such a preposterous notion.

Ned looked proudly at his two unlikely partners. "We will all have a great deal of things to think about and do before tomorrow morning when we will give our Blue Whale a final mission," he told them. "Lets sleep."

The morning light pierced the ocean's surface and made its way to the sleeping trio resting on the back of the Blue Whale. They looked around, making sure that no one had arrived to transport the Blue Whale away. Flop and Ned lifted the heavy jaw of the Blue Whale up as Eccoh slipped past the rows of baleen and settled on the seven hundred pound tongue that would make a proper cushion for their long stay in the mouth of this most unlikely escape vehicle.

On the count of three Flop and Ned coordinated a quick roll into the mouth of the whale as they settled on the tongue together. The darkness of the mouth gave them an eerie feeling as they realized that today was either their final day on Earth or the beginning of an incredible odyssey.

It wouldn't be long now before the many whales that were to be the pall bearers of the Blue came to deliver it to Megadon and his soldiers. Indeed, the sounds of activity were just now outside the mouth. To the horror of the trio inside someone was attempting to open it. After two or three attempts, a voice called out the their names.

"Hey!" it called. "Let me in. It's me. Kila." The trio quickly lifted the roof of the Blue Whale's mouth and opened it. In swam Kila, and the reunion was a happy moment for everyone, especially Flop who was almost in tears. They huddled there in the dark mouth of the whale hugging and playfully teasing Kila.

But their celebration was short lived as the body of the Blue Whale suddenly began to move. In silence the quartet separated and stretched out across the tongue of the giant whale, deciding to get some sleep as the pallbearers took the Blue Whale to its final resting place. When they awoke they would be forced to listen to the tearing of flesh as hundreds of ravenous sharks accepted the whale's final gift. It would also mark, either the beginning of the adventure of a lifetime, or certain death for them all.

Chapter Four

INTO THE JAWS OF DEATH

The returning Coast Guard helicopters were visible from the dock, and the thump of rotor blades echoed against the moored boats. The boats and helicopters had not found Ned. Miller stood forlornly at the end of the pier; an image of despair. His son was gone.

The commander of the Coast Guard walked toward him and touched his shoulder in a gesture of condolence. "They searched everywhere," he said. "But to no avail."

Many times it had been his sad duty to inform a grieving loved one of their loss. The sea is unforgiving and claims many lives. The professor stared into the water and the shadow of a large bird sent the tinker mackerel he was watching into a frantic retreat under the dock and out of the sight. He looked up and stared at the strange bird, unlike any other he had ever seen.

It was Dawinn, the same bird that delivered Ned into the ocean's depths. Their eyes locked as Dawinn swept to the nearest piling and summed up the dumbfounded professor. The professor's eyes showed the tears welling in his eyes while Dawinn offered a stern repose to this man who had mistreated Ned.

54

The creature spoke. "Ned is alive, and on his way to free the whales from the hunt," Dawinn said, then disappeared as a ball of diffusing light.

Like any father, Miller wanted to believe in the possibility that his son was still alive. He hoped that fate would give him the second chance to love his son. He allowed his hope to return, even though the news came from a mystical bird!

The laborious task of transporting the Blue Whale was nearly over. The territory of the Great Whites began to define itself with the shapes of long finned torpedoes filling the gray horizon. The pallbearers of this gargantuan offering tensed as they approached the mass of Great White Sharks. Although Megadon had never harmed the deliverers of any carcass, it was natural for the whales to be leery.

The tense atmosphere awakened Kila first, then Flop. Eccoh and Ned were cuddling together and were the last to awaken. Kila whispered to the others that they must be nearly there as he felt the clicks of fear coming from the dolphins that had accompanied the Blue Whale.

All movement stopped as the body of the massive Blue ground to a halt on the sandy sea bottom. The heartbeats of the four escapees made faint echoes off the walls of the baleen that shielded them from the hundreds of ravenous sharks. Time was suspended and within it, the strange silence deepened. The flow of current flushing through the cracks of the Blue Whales mouth was the only sound to be heard. As the tension mounted, the silence was broken by the sounds of a faint conversation. Kila had the best hearing so he was pushed forward to the very tip of the dead whale's mouth to listen. This is what he heard as the dolphin spoke.

"Honorable Megadon, we have once again delivered to you and yours a blessing in good faith from the spirit that is the fabric of all whales. We bequeath to you the carcass of a Blue Whale. This whale's soul has joined as one with that of the All Knowing. We know that if the sharks are strong the oceans will be healthy. We wish you well, sir," said the dolphin.

Megadon offered a blessing to the whales, which put them all at ease. He bade them farewell and wished them a good life. Out of a long standing respect for the whales, Megadon never let the festivities begin until they were out of sight. It was usually a quick departure!

The sharks began their ritual dance around the whale in final tribute to this once awesome sea creature, as Megadon was careful to keep a respectful dignity to all encounters. The dance and tribute came to a close as Megadon and a few of his top soldiers approached the head of the whale to begin another tradition that no live whale ever saw or knew of.

The tradition had always been to offer the greatest delicacy to the leader of the shark world. That leader, of course, was Megadon, and the delicacy was the tongue of the whale!

When Megadon was assured of the pallbearers' departure and the all-clear signal was given, the feast would begin. This message sparked another dance, one of a simulated attack where the open jaws of one hundred enormous mouths made mock attacks on different locations of the whale. Each shark moved into position to stake a claim to a certain part of the carcass. They became entitled to whatever section of whale they first passed over.

The sharks remained poised over their intended targets and waited for the signal to begin feeding. Megadon wouldn't hold them back any longer. They had to wait until he held the tongue in his mammoth mouth and circled his troops in a parade of celebration to life. Then their feast would begin. Three of Megadon's finest sharks began to lift the upper jaw of the Blue Whale so that Megadon could reach in with his imposing row of teeth and snag the tongue, beginning the feeding frenzy.

Many atmospheres of pressure weighted down the jaw and the three sharks motioned that they needed help opening the mouth. Reinforcements arrived just as Megadon gave a practice snap with his thirty-foot wide mouth. The closing mouth of Megadon caused a rush of water that assisted the sharks in breaking the suction of the mouth. It had seemed particularly difficult to open this whale's mouth, and the reason for this soon became obvious. As Megadon made the ritual darting for the tongue, he turned hard to the right of the jaw when he saw four creatures inside!

The entire community of sharks gathered around the entrance of the open mouth. There sat Flop, Eccoh and Ned trembling on the tip of the whale's tongue. Kila's wide eyes filled with terror, a sight not unnoticed by the hungry sharks. Kila shook from head to tail as he huddled in the middle of the whale's throat, ready to sink into the stomach rather than be eaten alive.

Megadon gave them such an evil stare that Kila nearly fainted on the spot. Luckily, he became lodged in the throat so that he couldn't fall into the belly of the whale. Eccoh was behind Ned and Flop was behind her as they froze in abject terror.

Things looked grim, to say the least, as Megadon edged closer. His eyes and upper row of teeth were inches from the trio perched on the tip of the tongue.

To the astonishment of Flop and Eccoh, Ned was able to speak. "Good morning, Megadon," he said.

The Great Leader of the world's ocean light stopped short, then fell back from the tongue in peals of laughter.

It wasn't what was said, but rather the way Ned looked that amused Megadon. He had never seen the likes of a boy with flippers and webbed feet resembling a dolphin before.

Megadon motioned for the others to be ready to feast, but before they were eaten, Megadon wished to give these interlopers time to explain themselves. Sharks began to gather near the mouth of the dead whale preparing to feast upon these new additions.

Megadon never took any of the fresh bounty other than

the tongue, so the jockeying began to take a new turn for Ned, Flop, Eccoh and Kila.

"Before you all meet your final fate," Megadon said, "I will grant you one chance to tell me how you have found yourselves in the mouth of our dinner."

Flop choked on his words and his garbled utterances were a source of delight to the nearby sharks. Eccoh nudged Ned and nuzzled up along side of him for moral support. Ned cleared his throat as bubbles from his efforts rose to the surface.

He began the tale of his father's boat and of their mission to find the migration secrets of the whales. This story fascinated Megadon, but it was obvious that those behind him were growing impatient. Gnashing teeth and jerking bodies made a nerve racking environment for Ned to concentrate while telling his story.

Megadon coaxed the threesome out of the whale's mouth and sent Eccoh to arouse Kila. Kila lifted his woozy head to see that his position in this mess hadn't changed. He fainted again. Kila was then pulled out of the throat of the whale by three sharks. They positioned him so he would be the first course when the feeding started.

At last, Ned finished his story and the tale of the Blue Whale. He explained how they intended to get by the sharks and find a way to save the whales. At this point, Ned was telling the story with the ease of someone relating all this to a boyhood friend. He had begun to feel a kinship with this thirty five million year old leader of the oceans.

The sharks were nervously awaiting to feast on the whale. Instead, Megadon left the misfits leaning on the sandy ocean floor against the open jaw, and began a leisurely swim around the Blue Whale.

"What is he thinking," they wondered. Megadon returned and looked to the patience-frayed sharks. He looked to Ned who seemed to be the leader of the group.

"I am sorry, Ned," he said. "But the law of the sea is such that I cannot offer you and your brave friends any protection from your fate. You have disturbed a place of sacred ritual. My love of my soldiers is going to take precedence over my intrigue with your plight. I am sorry, but my soldiers will escort you from here and they will no doubt do what they do naturally and consume all of you," Megadon ended sadly.

It seemed their fate was sealed as Megadon chose an escort party that gladly volunteered to lead them away and to be the recipient of four plentiful meals.

Ned yelled out to Megadon, "Good sir, I haven't told you all of the story yet."

Megadon turned to assure Ned he had heard enough and that nothing would change his mind. The escort sharks showed a smile of relief.

Ned shouted again as Megadon moved further from sight. "Megadon, we have come to deliver the Map of Currents and locate the Tooth."

All the sharks stopped cold. Megadon began the slow swim to the misfits with a most serious and stern expression on his face. "Ned, if you knew of the heartache I have suffered over my son, Naw, you would not toy with my good nature. For this you will no longer need an escort from this feast, but will be a part of it. Let it begin now," ordered Megadon.

He was obviously shaken by Ned's feeble attempt to avoid their fate. One large shark squirmed past the others and rested next to the ear of Megadon. His message caused the great leader to eye the foursome with astonishment.

Kila was still passed out and had missed the whole episode. In his sleep, he surely would have been the easiest of the misfits to eat.

Megadon turned to address the solders. "Faithful troops, you are all aware of the Map of Currents and the lost Tooth that has kept my beloved son, Naw, from me for a long time. Today we have heard this unlikely group of stowaways make an offer to challenge the Map of Currents and to find the Tooth. I intended to make an example of these invaders of our ritual, but I have learned that at the very moment when this boy- dolphin offered to attempt the actual Map of Currents came aglow. I believe this is a sign from the All Knowing.

"Come, and deliver these odd volunteers to my throne to prepare the Map of Currents so we can review it before their journey. Now we can begin the feast in our traditional ways!"

Ned called Megadon over and whispered what had to have been a question, then waited for an answer. After a moment Megadon gave Ned the oddest look. "Yes, Ned. It does," he said simply.

The misfits and Ned were taken to the ledge that Megadon meditated on each day. Ned and Eccoh exchanged loving looks.

Flop and Kila looked at Ned and called him an idiot. "You've volunteered us for a mission of certain death," said Flop.

"Do you realize Ned just saved you from certain death from these sharks?" Eccoh asked.

Flop didn't appreciate Eccoh's defense of Ned and argued that he'd rather go quickly at the jaws of Megadon's soldiers than to be tortured by the likes of Kratch and his troops.

The mention of Kratch eased the debate and Ned boldly asked for a minute to speak his piece. "I'm sorry I have placed you all in this predicament and I promise that none of you need assist me with the Map of Currents. When they set us free from here, you can return to the Ocean Haven. I'll continue on the route to free the Millennium Angel and Naw ... and hopefully eliminate Kratch for good.

"Furthermore," he boldly added, "when I do free the oceans of Kratch, I will come to get all of you to join me in swimming freely in this magic universe of water."

"Most of all, I wish to do this for Megadon and his son," Ned exclaimed.

Sitting behind the ledge, Megadon had been listening. He rose to the level of the sitting whales and greeted the misfits and Ned. He didn't let on that he had heard every word.

"Well," he said. "I see you are all comfortable and I trust that in the morning light you will be anxious to get on with the plan to find the Tooth and swim the gauntlet of challenges that Kratch has set in the Map Of Currents?"

"Why, yes, of course," said Flop, as the others nodded. Kila cowered and moved behind Flop.

"By the way," said Megadon. "As long as only one of you makes the choice to go in search of the Tooth and deliver the Map, the others can go as they please. I know what a dangerous undertaking this is. My son," he paused, "Naw, knew it all too well."

Megadon's voice was filled with sorrow as he spoke his son's name. Kila and Flop were ecstatic that they could choose their destiny without being eaten by sharks. The two of them were already discussing where they intended to visit first when they return to the Ocean Haven.

Eccoh curled herself next to Ned and told Flop and Kila that she planned to stay with Ned. Ned was deeply touched. He had never been in love, but suddenly his heart swelled with that emotion — a feeling he had never before felt.

"Even if it isn't love," Ned thought. "I don't care as long as it never stops."

Megadon swam to the surface where he would spend the night seeking a sign from the All Knowing. It didn't seem possible that the misfits below were capable of finding the lost Tooth or completing the mission of the Map of Currents, and certainly not of dodging Kratch and his ruthless army of Bullycudas. His soldiers would surely kill them just to please their leader.

Unfortunately, with their capture and demise, all hope for the ocean world of light would also die. Megadon was well aware of the approaching Millennium. He knew the Millennium Angel and his kingdom would come to an abrupt end if somebody didn't defeat the evil Kratch, but not a single soul had come forward since the capture of Naw.

Now, three misfit marine mammals and a funny looking underwater boy were about to undertake a task that all the valiant sharks had refused.

No sign from above arrived that night, and in the morning light, Megadon sank downward to focus on unfolding the Map of Currents before Ned, Flop, Eccoh and Kila.

Ned watched Megadon arrive and settle into the thick green weeds that matted the ledge. Ned swam over to the now sleeping legend. He curled up alongside the omnipotent presence and said a silent prayer for Megadon's son. After all, Ned knew that both he and Naw had one great thing in common: the overwhelming need to see their fathers' once again.

In the black hole of Kratch's domain, Naw's anguish had been unbearable. At the very moment Ned began his prayer, a ball of light pierced Naw's forehead. The intensity sent Naw reeling backward in a somersault. As he righted himself, he was filled with light and renewed hope.

That light affected more than just Naw. Kratch felt a painful jolt in the open hole where Megadon's Tooth had been lodged. Kratch only winced and felt that Megadon must be up to some magic, or was preparing to rescue his son. Kratch became very curious.

Megadon arose early to review the Map Of Currents with Naw's best friend, Snap. In the distance two undistinguishable shapes began to approach Megadon and his most trusted soldier. Megadon knew who it was and why they were here. It was the toothless shark, Lonah, and his father.

Lonah's father made a customary gesture of respect to Megadon as they drew near. "Honorable Megadon, I come to offer my son, Lonah, to assist the whales and the dolphin boy in their quest."

"What, sir," Megadon asked , "do you feel your son can contribute to this already questionable troop of volunteers?"

"Well, sir," piped in Lonah, "I, too, have had little to live for here in the oceans, since I have no teeth. Like the others I simply wish to prove I am a worthy soul.

"That is most noble, Lonah, most noble," replied Megadon, pausing in reflection. "If the boy dolphin agrees, you may go."

Lonah was squirming with excitement as he had always been left out of all the normal things other sharks did, and had to count on his father for all his food.

"You can return here as soon as I send for you, Lonah — after we consult with the boy.

Lonah swam ahead of his father who then turned to Megadon. "Do you think they have a chance, Megadon?" he inquired.

"All of life is a chance, good sir," he told the worried father. "We, as fathers can only hope that this opportunity is a good and worthy one." Megadon returned to study the Map.

Together, he and Snap tried to pin down the most likely place to find the Tooth. Without the Tooth, the mission could not be completed. Ned and the others awoke with the nervous anticipation all great adventurers feel. Kila and Flop were excited about the idea of going home. Eccoh and Ned talked bravely and spent much time gazing into each other's eyes; caring little about the real danger they were about to face. Kila and Flop could see that the two of them were falling in love and Flop began to sob.

"What is wrong with you?" asked Kila.

Flop whimpered with emotion. "If we leave Eccoh and Ned now," he told Kila, "Then we might be the ones who ruin their love because we weren't there to help when they needed us."

"You mean that you're willing to give up your life for the love of these two, Flop?" Kila asked.

"Look at them, Kila, and tell me that your love for our dearest friend, Eccoh, isn't more important than our own empty purpose here on Earth?"

Kila looked over at the two, swimming in a tight circle with a flipper over each other's backs. The smiles and embraces of Eccoh with her newfound love convinced a reluctant Kila, and he agreed to join the misfits. Having decided to join in, Kila trembled with fear as he thought about the future.

Megadon and Snap joined Ned, and the misfits to give them a briefing of the Map and the possible location of the Tooth. He wanted to give the whales one more chance to back out. Part of him hoped that they would decline to go. He knew they were no match against Kratch and the challenges they faced. But, Megadon also recognized that no others had come forth to free the Millennium Angel, Naw, or fight to free the oceans of the evil Kratch. Time was running out. The misfits were the only hope.

Megadon greeted the awaiting misfits. He and the other sharks had decided Ned was a whale of different sorts, but a whale nonetheless.

The participants all gathered into a tight circle as Megadon orchestrated the seating arrangements. He placed Ned directly to his right where he held the rolled Map of Currents tightly to his side. Megadon began addressing the group that included Ned, Eccoh, Kila, Flop, and Snap. Moving into the circle were two sharks that were unknown to Ned and company.

"Before we get to the Map of Currents," Megadon began, "I would like to introduce Lonah, the son of one of our greatest warriors. Lonah would like to be with you on this perilous mission. And I would consider it a favor to me if you would consider having him."

"Honorable Megadon," Ned asked. "Can you give us one good reason to have this shark along on our pursuit to complete the Map of Currents?"

Before they even heard an answer from Megadon, Lonah smiled, revealing that he hadn't one single tooth in his head. Kila and Flop began to laugh, as did Snap.

"What an absurd sight," said Kila. "A Great White Shark with no teeth."

Lonah turned fast to swim away from this embarrassment, but Ned yelled to him, "Lonah come back, you are most welcome and needed in this quest." Ned recognized Lonah's retreat as the same one he had made so many times aboard the *Krill*.

Lonah looked downward, still feeling the sting of shame over his physical defect. Ned swam to him and poked his leathery sides and squeezed at his muscle, while nodding approval at what a fine physical specimen Lonah was.

The light and sparkle returned to Lonah's eyes as he swam to the now jittery Kila. After all, getting next to Great White sharks wasn't what Killer Whales usually do.

Megadon smiled upon the entire gathering as Lonah struggled to get comfortable. Lonah's awkward charm began to win over the uneasy misfits. His toothless smile was quite engaging and his friendly demeanor posed no threat.

A silence fell over them as Megadon spoke. "As I begin," he said, "I will offer you all the opportunity to rescind your offer to undertake this mission." He watched to assess their reaction.

Kila looked around to see if any others would be willing to quit. All he saw was firm resolve.

"Well," went on Megadon. "Before we discuss the map or the possible location of the Tooth, do you have any questions?"

Flop raised his thirteen foot flipper. "Why haven't you gone to save your son, Naw?"

Megadon sighed and said, "Many times I have begun the mission to rescue my son and many times I have set out in the darkest hours of the night to search for the Tooth. And many times I have cried over the son I've lost. Yet, every time I begin this journey the spirit of my son holds me back. If Kratch were to engage me at any point of this endeavor, he has the one thing in his grasp that could compromise my power. He has my son.

"So you see, Flop, when my son's spirit meets mine, it always asks me the same question: What kind of leader or father would I be if I let one shark, be it my son or not, become more important than the light of the oceans? So we are relying on all of you. Henceforth you will no longer refer to yourselves as misfits, but as the Warriors of Light."

"I have a question," said Kila. "What was it that Ned asked you when you set us free from the feast. Megadon looked to Ned for approval and Ned nodded.

"Ned asked me if the Map Of Currents led to the place where men kill whales," Megadon said.

All eyes were on Ned as a sheepish smile filled his face. "I believe we can still save the whales as part of our quest," he said gently. "... don't you?"

Chapter Five

THE MAP OF CURRENTS

The Millennium Angel's cave had become a dark prison, and in the darkness her spirit languished as her light grew dim. Her wings drooped and her long flowing hair rested unmoving on the floor of the cave. She was dying. Soon her spirit would depart, her mission of light unfulfilled.

Megadon and the others were not aware of the angel's plight. Ned and the newly ordained 'Warriors of Light' would have to move swiftly to rescue her. Time, Kratch, and the dangers of the Map Of Currents were overwhelming challenges for Ned, Eccoh, Kila, Flop, and Lonah.

Back at the dock, commercial fishermen loaded crates of fresh bait as handsomely dressed yatchsmen and their children prepared for a fun day of sailing. The weather was sunny and calm — ideal for those fortunate to have free time to sail.

To the anxiety-filled Professor Miller, the crowd was like an unwanted swarm of mosquitoes. The activity of the others thwarted his desperate efforts to find Ned. Along for the mission, Professor Conway joined him in the search.

Ned's father's pace was frantic, and his manners became razor thin as he pushed past the last yachtsman, whom he intentionally bumped into the water. Miller never even stopped to apologize. The anxious professor climbed atop his motor vessel and started the engines. The sounds of the *Krill's* engines echoed throughout the marina as the boat made way to the open ocean.

A spray of cold salty sea washed over the two professors. Conway found it refreshing. For Miller it was a flash of pain as he thought of the waves that washed over his son before he was lost to the sea. Another wave swept over the rails narrowly missing the two. The search for Ned had begun.

In the dark and devilish world of Kratch an air of excitement filled the waters. A meeting of the most evil allies of Kratch was about to take place. Their purpose was to set plans into action that would foil the mission of the Warriors of Light. The control of the ocean world was closer to the reach of Kratch.

Entering the confines of Kratch's domain were some of the ocean's most notorious allies. Thousands of Bullycudas were escorting the lot of them into the midnight darkness of Kratch's lair.

First to arrive under the careful protection of the Bullycudas was the bitter and dreaded Tentacle, a sixty foot giant squid, that insisted on eating nothing but whales. Tentacle was the victim of a vicious attack by a sperm whale when he was a young father. The attack didn't kill

Tentacle, but his only son was carried off during the attack. Tentacle vowed to kill any whale, especially every sperm whale that crossed his path as revenge for his son. It is said his territory bordered upon the favored calving grounds, and that many females and their calves have been Tentacle's victims. Tentacle would squirt miles of jet black ink into the waters to confuse the young whales. When he captured them, he would lure the mothers into mortal danger as they responded to the cries of the calves.

Tentacle was interested in the power and prestige of being the second most nefarious leader in the evil ocean. A menacing figure, his tentacles were seventy feet long, and atop his head were large squinted eyes and numerous scars. Streams of ink oozed from his appendages as he neared the opening to Kratch's hole. Tentacle turned to give a nod of thanks to Kratch's Bullycudas as he slithered slowly into the pitch dark pit.

Following Tentacle was the King of the Giant Worms, Zid. He was the last vestige of the ocean dinosaurs that still lived in the mysterious ocean's depths. The Giant Worms bored deep holes into the ocean floor, enabling them to survive the eons of change. Their victims rarely saw these Giant Worms as they hid in their holes, and very few of their prey escaped to tell of their hiding places. At night the bones of the victims were dragged many miles away and scattered on the ocean floor.

Zid was the king of this ancient order of predators, and his queen stayed at home as she was expected to lay eggs soon. This would produce hundreds of offspring ensuring the survival of the Giant Worms as a species. She only laid eggs every hundred years, so missing one litter could mark the end of these dangerous underwater creatures. Zid's head was rounded, and many warts covered his eyes, cheeks and mouth. A continuous flow of slime seeped from his skin causing a long grey slick in his wake.

The cruel looking Zid hissed constantly at the Bullycudas that accompanied him. They were wary of his deceitful ways, and they knew Zid feared no one, not even Kratch. An easy meal if Zid got hungry, they kept a safe distance from him as he slithered down the edge of the hole with a slow deliberation.

Far from Kratch, the Warriors of Light gathered round Ned, who sensed they were feeling overwhelmed at the enormous task before them. Kila muttered to himself that he should have stayed at the Haven, and Flop shook his head at Ned in the most unflattering way. Lonah reflected happily upon his newfound mission, while Eccoh and Ned cuddled and giggled at the absurdity of the whole mess they were in.

Megadon was feeling better about Ned. As a result of his many years as the sole administrator of the light in the oceans he had become a fine judge of potential leaders. Megadon's gaze softened as he stared down at Ned. It was this same look he had given Naw the day he left with the map and the now-lost Tooth.

Snap rolled open the Map of Currents. Time had worn the edges and the salty water had softened the features of the map to create a fuzzy appearance in certain areas. The map was surprisingly detailed in its depiction of the ocean's bottom. Ned was impressed by the vividness of the mountainous areas and the sandy flats that resembled a desert leading to more mountains and valleys.

As he thought of the many happy hours he and his dad had spent pouring over charts, he realized that the change in their relationship started when his mom died. Ned missed his mother, and had tried hard to understand his father. Still he couldn't shake the idea that he wasn't good enough.

Megadon asked Snap to tell the story of the loss of the Tooth before he briefed them on the map and the direction they must take. Snap told of his journey with Naw, and of how they had easily passed the Burrows of the Giant Worms. He told Ned and the others that they felt powerful and secure because they trusted and believed in the All Knowing. Naw had said the mission would be easy because the All Knowing would be with them all the way. During their passage through the Canyons of Perpetual Darkness, Snap and Naw realized the error of their thinking. He described their last moments together and pointed to the last location in this dreaded place where the Tooth should be.

Kila felt faint and began to tremble. Snap looked upset as he recalled his last moments with Naw. Ned held his flipper over Snap's back offering a kindly touch to comfort him.

Megadon then asked Snap to describe the Canyon Of Perpetual Darkness to indicate where the Tooth might be found.

"There are many strange rocks that surround the Canyon," he said. "The colors there are very beautiful and are populated with many fish."

"Are the reefs coral?" Ned asked.

"Yes," said Megadon, "they are. Oddly enough, Kratch has indicated in the map that they extend well into the canyon, despite a lack of light."

Snap then went on to tell of Kratch's lair and how the deepest, darkest place in the canyon is where Kratch is forced to hide from the light. "We know that even the slightest light is excruciatingly painful to him," Snap said. "Unfortunately, this darkest spot is where the Tooth was dropped. Without light, it will be almost impossible to find."

This was not encouraging news for the tales' spellbound adventurers. Ned worried about the impact of the overwhelming odds on his friends, and asked Snap if he would like to join them.

Megadon announced that he could not allow Snap to go, and no one dared to ask why. Megadon thanked Snap for his briefing. Snap offered each of the five bewildered pioneers his blessings and swam off.

Megadon gazed at and pointed to a spot on the map.

"Let's begin here, since you are closest to this place. Within a day's journey you will enter the source of our life's force. I believe you call it the current, Ned. It is these currents that carry all life, and in your case it could carry you to your death."

Kila keeled over in a faint again, and Flop had to come and steady him.

Megadon became impatient, and was about to ask them to remove Kila, as he awoke and rejoined the group's discussion. Megadon's stern look was all Kila needed for him to realize that he had better not faint again.

Megadon continued. "The current can fool you and force you to drift unknowingly into harm's way. The Burrows of the Giant Worms is very dangerous because the worms are well camouflaged. If they get hold of you, it will mean a slow and certain death."

"Why do you say 'slow death', Megadon?" asked Lonah.

Megadon continued. "They tie themselves in tight knots, then hold you until you are too weak to struggle. Then they begin to eat you a little at a time. Some like to wait until the flesh has rotted before they begin."

Kila began to feel as if he were going to faint again. Flop nudged him sharply.

"The last ones to engage in any confrontation will be the King and Queen. They are the only ones capable of producing offspring for the future. They come into the open only to eat or escape. The likelihood of their needing escape is slim, as they are well guarded, and their tunnels many directions, making it difficult for predators to find them.

"If these creatures beset you, be sure that someone escapes with the Map Of Currents. Once you have passed the Burrows of the Giant Worms, you will come to the Canyons of Perpetual Darkness. As you know, this is where Kratch captured Naw. Here your mission will be in great peril, for here you may encounter Kratch. Any light will hinder his ability to lead his Bullycudas in capturing you."

"Is there ever any light in the Canyons, Megadon?" asked Eccoh.

"We are approaching an unusual time of year when the light is abundant there," Megadon explained. "This period passes quickly. We will sense its arrival when it comes, but we never know exactly what time it is going to be."

"How do you suggest we go about avoiding Kratch while we are in the Canyons," asked Flop.

"Kila is your great hope here since he can detect all movement," Megadon suggested. "With him as your scout, perhaps you can avoid the Bullycudas.

"The only reason I have allowed this coward to assist you in this dangerous quest is because of these special abilities. If Kila fails, then you fail with him." Megadon sternly eyed the now shivering Kila. It was the first time an angry or judgmental word had been spoken by Megadon.

Kila was mortified when called a coward, and struggled to hold back tears.

Megadon suddenly looked at and charged at Kila, his

thirty foot mouth agape, and seven rows of razor sharp teeth showing.

Kila fainted.

Megadon turned sharply to avoid any contact with Kila because Eccoh made a high pitched sound, forcing Megadon to turn suddenly. She berated Megadon for his harsh behavior.

Oddly enough, her reaction seemed to please Megadon. He let her finish the tirade and then addressed them all as Kila was awakened by Eccoh's high pitched squeals. "My spirited Warriors of Light," he began. "I do not wish to hurt or alarm you, but what you have just experienced is but a small sampling of the terror you will encounter in the world of Kratch and his Bullycudas.

"Remember! When Kratch comes at you like I did, he will finish the job."

Megadon then addressed Kila. "You are the weak link in this pursuit, and if you cannot help them, you must stay here or return to the Ocean Haven."

Kila moved forward and stuttered as he looked at his friends. "Uh ... I don't know if I can do this gang. If you want me to, I will go back to the Haven."

Lonah moved quickly to the center of the circle and said that he felt Kila would be essential to their success. He believed that Kila would come through for them when the moment was right. The rest beamed at Lonah. He had found a place of love and respect in the hearts of the Warriors of Light.

"The final phase of your quest is to find the Tooth," Megadon continued. "This entire endeavor will be meaningless without it. As you near the end of the Map of Currents, Kratch will be desperate to find and kill you all.

"I have reflected upon how Kratch will respond if he hears that you have found the Tooth. He will call all his allies and Bullycudas to force you into battle to the death. He will do anything to rid the world of the Light. Only your courage and resolve will bring victory."

He asked them to form a circle and touch fins in silence. Each one asked the All Knowing for help in that moment. In the circle of oneness, they realized that together they were more powerful than they could know.

Megadon broke the circle, and his final words to the Warriors of Light were these: "I do not know what the future holds for you, but your courage is something I shall never forget. I will call upon the All Knowing on every new evening for your success. If I can be reunited with my son I will be forever in your debt. The All Knowing cannot be there for you at all times but he has given me the power to give you each a gift.

"To the whales, I give gills — giving you the ability to breath underwater. This will be useful in hiding or escaping detection from your enemies.

"To Lonah, who already is equipped with these gills, will be given the power of genius. His thoughts may come to save one or all of you. This is the most the All Knowing can offer except his desire to see you succeed. That will be up to you, and only you! Now go and find your destiny, Warriors of Light!"

Slowly the five Warriors of Light swam away from the mighty Megadon. Looking back, they knew the security and peaceful life they had had, was now in the past.

On the surface of the ocean, far from Ned, the *Krill* had just passed a pod of whales. The usual excitement over such a sight was overshadowed by the grief of Professor Miller. He stared vacantly at the sea as he relived the events on the night Ned went overboard. He realized if he hadn't been so mean, his son would never have had to hide at the stern and cry. Miller shook himself from the nightmare and went back to the pilot house to steer onward to find his son.

The *Krill* disappeared into the horizon as night set in on the two man crew. The captain at the helm of the suddenly felt a jolt of hope. His entire being shook. Miller looked out the window to see the strange bird pass the port side and disappear in a ball of light. He began to weep silently in gratitude.

Kratch was also busy preparing for an encounter with Ned. In his murky and decrepit cavern, the Lord of Darkness was planning to catch and eliminate the Warriors of Light. Finding out through spies of the gang of misfits heading to conquer the forces of ocean evil, and knowing he held Megadon's son as a prisoner, Kratch could almost taste his victory.

He had been meeting with his greatest allies: Zid, the King of the Giant Worms; Tentacle, the Great Squid; and General Slash. The meeting stressed the need to organize their forces so that the Warriors of Light would fail.

Zid was the first to leave the meeting. He was immediately escorted by hundreds of Bullycudas back to the Burrows of the Giant Worms.

The next to leave was Tentacle. He was chosen to back the others should the new warriors survive the initial challenges of the Map of Currents.

Next General Slash emerged to hover near Kratch's pit of sand and secrets.

Unbeknownst to Kratch, there was another observer to the meeting. Overseeing the clandestine meeting was the Jellyfish Wizard. He was hidden in the confines of a hollowed coral reef where his secret hideaway lay. He had a round crystal ball filled with blue gray water unlike that surrounding him. A magic mix made especially for seeing the world from afar, even Kratch was unaware of the Wizard's ability.

The Wizard watched carefully as the meeting went on. The last look in the crystal ball was that of the General coming into the forefront. The Jellyfish Wizard watched gleefully as the General took one last look down into the pitch black to see the large whites of Kratch's eyes staring back at him. They were twin moons glowing bright and full of vengeance for Megadon. Even General Slash registered a twinge of fear as he swam out of Kratch's view.

The Wizard now focused in on the Millennium Angel. Her light was fading as the darkness continued to weaken her. The flow of water no longer penetrated the dark cave, and gone was the glow that had shown so brightly the day Spikes discovered her. The Wizard knew that her light and life would soon end if no one came to her rescue.

One last image filled the Wizard's crystal ball. Three tiny jellyfish swam aimlessly in a dark and dreary place. They seemed very unhappy and their eyes were sunken in despair. The Wizard bent over their image. "I'm coming my loved one's," he whispered. "Don't fret. I'm coming!"

Chapter Six
WHALE OF A DILEMMA

The warm waters and gentle currents delighted the five adventurers. They were pleased to be able to unwind from the stress of recent days, and these currents became the voluminous hands massaging their tension filled bodies. Ned began to detect patterns in the bottom topography, which his father had spoken of many times. Despite all his misgivings, Ned had to admit that his father had always been a dedicated teacher.

As they progressed toward the Map of Currents, Ned noticed they were approaching a series of high bottom cliffs. He knew them as areas of something called an 'upwelling'. This meant that it was extremely possible that food was plentiful. Ned remembered his father telling him that an upwelling was when the sea's bottom rose sharply, exposing a series of small underwater mountain ranges or ledges that allowed plants and nutrients to mix and fertilize, producing food for fish. This would, and does, create plant food for the microscopic life forms that are the core of life in the oceans.

Indeed, plankton was abounding, hitching a free ride in the currents, while grazing for essential nutrients to survive. Seeing this underwater miracle took Ned's breath away. He was witnessing the workings of the ocean life chain first hand. He no longer had to imagine what the life forms his father had talked of. Ned had become a part of the chain of life; he was linked to Mother Ocean. He felt privileged and grateful.

Ned marveled at the high rising layers of sand and deposits of clay mixed with minerals that had been bulldozed by the last glaciers of over 25,000 years ago. Schools of fish moved in perfect unity, traversing the vast collection of algae and creating a laser light show of luminescence at the slightest disturbance in the water column. The scene was electric, as everywhere Ned looked neon lighted plants sparkled. Certainly only something the All Knowing could have conceived.

The morning was a glorious one. Light filtered to the bottom and bounced back to highlight the plankton, crustaceans and the millions of small fish whose scales sparkled like diamonds as they passed by. Eccoh, Kila, Flop and Lonah marveled at the beauty and bounty of this magic in motion. Moreover, they were filled with the joy of freedom, for this was the first time they ever swum as freely beyond the confines of Ocean Haven.

Kila was by now especially hungry, and Flop could hear the loud gurgles as his stomach complained. Lonah felt that primordial desire to hunt that was instinctive to all sharks as he watched the schools of fish pass by. Ned and Eccoh were somewhat oblivious to the need for food as they swam together touching flippers and flirting. Ned's ation with Eccoh finally gave way to the knowledge that they had better eat or they would be unable to challenge Kratch's Bullycudas, never mind the Lord of Darkness himself.

Ned announced that it was time to feed and asked Lonah to lead the charge. A look of helplessness filled them all. This was the first time any of them had done anything except wait for another whale to corral food into Ocean Haven to them. Lonah had always been forced to wait for whatever his father and brothers dropped directly in front of him. Ned suggested that they all pause for a moment and think it all through.

"Look," said Ned. "If we work together to confuse the fish and then corral them we can catch as many as we need."

Flop looked confused.

Ned explained that if they circle the fish in a unified way long enough, the schooling instincts would be overshadowed by total confusion. Then they could sweep in and eat.

It made perfect sense and Lonah began the process immediately with Flop, Eccoh, Ned and a reluctant Kila trailing behind. They targeted a nearby school of mackerel that was pursuing a school of eels. Lonah made the first pass at the unsuspecting fish. As the fish turned to the left to escape there was Flop, then Eccoh to the right and Ned on Flop's tail to close the circle.

Kila hung back, looking inadequate and embarrassed.

The fish were indeed dumbfounded and Lonah quickly gulped a mouthful. The others began feeding too and soon found their hunger subsided and their bellies felt better.

This is so easy! thought Flop. He took a mouthful and dumped it in front of Kila who didn't hesitate to gobble down the fish he was afraid to catch. When the school was gone, the mood was triumphant. They realized that they were truly a team and had experienced their first hunt.

"Shall we travel now or eat?" asked Ned.

They all chose to eat. Ned sensed from the fish that they were aware of their intentions, and suggested a new strategy might be in order.

"Flop," asked Ned. "Can you blow bubbles?"

"Why of course I can, Ned," replied Flop. "You've seen me do it."

"Good," said Ned. "Then you will provide the next feeding opportunity for us."

"How do you think I can do that, Ned?" asked Flop.

Ned began to tell them of a technique he had seen many times, called 'bubble feeding'.

"You see, Flop," explained Ned. "If you swim below the fish in tight circles, blow bubbles as fast and hard as you can, the cylindrical rise of bubbles corrals the fish just as we just did with our bodies."

"Then what?" asked Kila.

"Well," said Ned, matter of factly. "Then we all follow Flop into the wall of bubbles, all the way to the surface, and eat the fish inside on the way up."

The foursome at Ned's side laughed at the notion that the fish would tolerate such a procedure, but Ned asked them to try it.

They swam just below Flop as he initiated a tight, circular pattern of bubble blowing below the first school of fish. Finishing the circle, Flop charged through the middle of the column. Soon, to the astonishment of them all, fish were jammed in and drooping from every mouth.

Every mouth but Kila's! He hadn't made the charge with them, and Lonah and Eccoh gave him food. Kila worried Ned, who was fast emerging as the true leader of the group. Ned wondered how severe a danger the scared and seemingly unchangeable Killer Whale posed for the group and their mission. He kept silent about his concerns.

"Come," he said instead, not wishing to dampen the air of happiness in the group. "We have a long way to travel. Before we go any further, let's locate our position on the Map of Currents."

Ned held the legendary Map tightly to his side as the other four members of the journey gathered around him. Ned unraveled it before them as they gathered close together. Kila found a spot next to Lonah, deciding that any Great White Shark that would share his food with a Killer Whale couldn't be all bad.

Ned pointed to the next destination: the Canyons of Perpetual Darkness. A place rich in mystery, Ned went over the fact that the Burrows of the Giant Worms skirted that destination. He made it clear that as long as they kept their bearings, no trouble from the worms would be necessary. Kratch was on the lookout for them, but after finding the Tooth and passing through the canyons, they would only have to face Kratch.

He made it sound so easy. The Warriors of Light looked confident and as Ned rolled the Map, Flop began to lead the way to the canyons.

They all followed and swam for hours. Ned suddenly yelled for them to hold up and he pointed to a deep sandy valley that lay just beyond the underwater mountain range. It was nightfall and they were all tired.

"This is where we will rest tonight before we make the day's swim to the canyons, and we will all take guard to see that none of us drift with the currents that Megadon warned would push us into the path of certain death."

Flop suggested that since they were leaving the feeding grounds, they should polish off a few more schools of fish. Before Ned could say a word, a school of herring passed above. Flop led the charge, blowing bubbles, as Eccoh followed in direct pursuit. Lonah wrapped his mouth around Kila's tail and forced him to the center of the action, much to the chagrin of Kila.

Ned gleefully watched, as he was stuffed from the last feed. He knew the voracious appetite whales had, and also recognized that he and Eccoh needed far less than Flop, Kila, or especially Lonah, who like other sharks, were eating machines.

Again, the bubble net had done a magnificent job of

corralling the fish, and even Kila came through with a great mouthful of fish. At the surface, the sight of the neon green plants sparked an onslaught of birds, taking advantage of the many fragmented, confused, and discarded fish.

The bubble feeding continued, and Ned noticed that it was Lonah who kept Kila from leaving the feeding frenzy. Kila was actually feeding and chasing fish all by himself. By the end of the afternoon, Ned was certain he had seen Kila blow a circle of bubbles.

With the evening drawing near Ned realized they had better get to their designated resting spot soon. They knew that they faced the challenge of a lifetime in the Canyons Of Perpetual Darkness.

An air of frivolity and pride seemed to overshadow a fear of the unknown as they all settled down for the evening. They chatted freely about their first day and how the Warriors of Light had fooled the schools of fish using only bubbles. The children who had taken a giant step in overcoming their frailties and doubts were proud.

As each one experienced their success, and reveled in the most triumphant time of their lives, they began to see themselves differently. Their self confidence grew by leaps, and new vistas of opportunity seemed to open up before them. Flop started to think that even without being able to breach that he could probably be one of the other whales.

Lonah, too, sensed he had cheated himself by never trying to strike out on his own. This, he realized was a mistake. To Ned, it was a miracle to see the whole group react as a team, something that would be essential to survival during the next few days.

Ned noticed a wreck of a ship ahead and began to think of his father and the *Krill*. His thoughts drifted back to a time when his mother was alive and they were on the beach together. He imagined the faded red cedar and wire fences, bent from time, and the weight of shifting sands, and the paths through the dunes. He recalled the sounds of terns as they dove in protest at the heads of intruding crows and hawks intent on taking their precious young ones from their nests. Ned's father always kept him and his mother at a distance from the nesting birds.

Ned's reverie continued as he remembered his father and mother holding his hands on either side, and lifting him above the water as the tide rolled past their feet. He would giggle and they responded with the loving smiles of indulgent parents. It had been a wonderful time.

As Ned neared the sunken ship, he peered through the windows to see what he might learn of the voyage the crew had been on. The rusted beams and hollowed voids in the ship didn't hold many clues. The name of the ship had been peeled free of the hull by an incessant sanding of the tides.

As Ned moved on, his thoughts turned to his mother dying and his father choking back the tears as he sat by her side.

At that moment, Lonah engulfed him in his huge toothless jaws and woke Ned from his daydream. "Ned, you're going the wrong way," Lonah warned.

Ned shook his dolphin-like form and stretched, thanking Lonah for bringing him back to the present. As he moved to follow Lonah, now heading in the right direction, he whispered: "I love you, mom. And I love you too, dad."

Eccoh sensed Ned's melancholy and came to his side and stoked him with her flipper as they swam along. Ned's returning gaze penetrated the depths of her soul, leaving them both shaken. Eccoh broke away from Ned and breached at the surface.

They arrived at the sandy valley that Ned had chosen to rest for the evening. The timing was perfect, as the emotional highs, mixed with hundreds of pounds of digested fish had taken its toll. Ned explained the concept of taking watch before anyone settled in for the night.

The valley was a deep, soft, sandy crevice that lay just below the steep rise of sand similar to where they had caught fish. It just happened to be close to the mouth of the Canyon of Perpetual Darkness. Ned explained that he and Lonah would take the first watch while the others slept. Lonah also assured them he would herd them in a tight knit circle if they began to drift. No one wanted to drift into the Burrows of the Giant Worms. Kila was already asleep before any of this news was given. Ned told Flop and Eccoh they would be the next shift before they too fell asleep. The next day of travel would deliver them to the treacherous Canyons.

Flop, Kila, and Eccoh nestled tight to a curve of where the valley and the bottom connected. They looked so serene as Lonah hovered over them, as if they were his own children. The waters were especially warm in that valley as Ned figured it must be the gathering place of two great bodies of water. Ned and Lonah were as tired as the others but agreed to fight off sleep for the sake of the others. The two of them kept an eye on the sleeping brood as they hunkered down into the sand to keep watch. The warm water current started to affect Ned and Lonah and they felt sleepy.

Suddenly a wall of tiny bubbles filled their line of vision. As they stared at the bubbles they started to form very distinct shapes. First a Great White Shark appeared that looked exactly like Lonah. Then the shape of Kila, Flop, Ned and Eccoh. It was a hypnotic show that had Lonah and Ned so mesmerized that they never noticed that the sleeping Warriors of Light had disappeared. The caricatures of bubbles burst simultaneously in an explosion of fizz. This snapped Ned and Lonah in to a dizzy spell followed by an uncontrollable need to sleep. The two hit the sand in a deep coma.

The bubbles faded and exposed the huge demonic smile of the Jellyfish Wizard. He proceeded to gently wrap his tentacles around each of the sleeping warriors, peeling them apart and spinning them into the current adrift. First Eccoh, then Kila and lastly, Flop. Oddly, he left Lonah and Ned right where they had fallen asleep.

The other Warriors floated peacefully, still in a deep sleep. They seemed powerless to wake themselves and stop the roll into harm's way. They floated to the top of the valley that was the only barrier separating them from the Burrows of the Giant Worms.

Inch by inch the bodies of the Warriors of Light began to creep to the top and roll over the peak. One by one they careened over the mineral packed top of the valley, and one by one, they rolled over and into the reach of the Giant Worms.

Back in the valley, Lonah was in the deepest sleep of his life. His fertile mind led him into his painful past. He remembered a day with his father, Woden. A fine teacher, one day the two were swimming through a myriad of kelp in search of seals. Fluorescent blues and the yellows of abalone shone from the bottom where otters wedged open shells that they would lay on their stomachs before eating.

On this day, Woden was taking Lonah to the kelp to find other prey: the seals themselves. Ahead, Woden pointed out the playful, carefree creatures performing underwater ballets. Lonah found the dance tantalizing. Woden pressured Lonah to go for the seal and eat it, and Lonah never forgot that moment. His father had let him go by himself to catch his first meal. Lonah moved just beyond the sight of his father, hiding behind a massive collection of kelp as he surveyed his prey. Two or three seals now played out this dance of joy they portrayed in the kelp.

Lonah simply watched, unable to disrupt the playful seals. When he returned to his father to report that they had all escaped, he had lied. Woden knew it, and refused to feed or speak to his son for over a week. Lonah was almost dead from starvation and shame. When at his weakest point, Woden delivered enough food to him to bring him back to life. The father in Woden was stronger than the teacher, and, from that point on, the routine never changed. Lonah ate what was given to him, not captured by him.

Lonah awoke with a jolt from his dream, where the last vision was of a bull seal that had a distinct streak of orange meshed over his eye and ear. When he awakened he was pleased to see his friend, Ned. Lonah nudged Ned awake and the two of them smiled. Simultaneously they looked to see how Eccoh, Kila, and Flop were doing.

The trio were gone!

Ned and Lonah panicked. They looked everywhere within a few hundred yards of where the others were fast asleep. No one was in sight.

"Do you remember the Jellyfish that appeared before we went out?" Ned asked Lonah,

"Yes, I can still see his face. And the bodies of Flop, Eccoh and Kila were right beside the Jellyfish Wizard."

"You know who that was, Lonah?"

"Yes, Ned," said Lonah. "All the ocean creatures know of him and his evil. He must have taken the other Warriors to Kratch. The Jellyfish Wizard is an ally of evil, and can create illusions, as you have witnessed. Illusions that can cost you your life."

"Oh no, wait," cried Ned. "If he wanted us dead, why would he leave us?"

"I don't understand it, Ned, but I think we will find out."

Suddenly, screams were heard. A high pitched squeal of horror filled the valley as Flop's unmistakable screech reverberated clearly through the water.

Lonah and Ned realized they had better jump into action. They raced over the top of the valley to the rescue. Ned and Lonah were quickly closing in on their threatened friends.

The scene they found was horrifying. Giant Worms had captured Kila, Flop and Eccoh. To prevent their escape, they knotted themselves around their victims. Ned could see that the burrows interconnected and noticed that several worms had knotted themselves together, and like a ribbon of flesh, using the burrows to anchor them. They tightened the string on the now helpless trio of victims. Eccoh looked up to see Ned and Lonah approaching, and her eyes widened with hope. Her eyes met Ned's and he was overcome with rage.

As they approached Eccoh, the worms snarled and their heads twisted in fury. When they were ten feet from Eccoh, the King of the Giant Worms appeared and was poised, about to strike Ned. Lonah noticed King Zid just in time and rammed him, saving Ned from certain death.

Next, he swiftly engulfed the dolphin boy in his tooth-less grip and swam hurriedly to the safety of the valley where they had slept. In the distance they could still hear the cries of Eccoh, Flop and Kila.

Lonah released Ned from his grip and waited in silence as Ned recovered from his escape and dizzying ride to safety. He was very angry and upset and yelled at Lonah for interfering with the attempted rescue.

Lonah let Ned spout off before replying. "Ned, you were inches from the striking mouth of Zid. If he ate you and took the map then we would all be doomed.

"You see, Ned, the Giant Worms will be counting on a foolish attempt to save Kila, Flop, and Eccoh, and will keep them alive as long as we have the Map of Currents."

Ned calmed down immediately and realized that Lonah was right. He was grateful to this Great White Shark. Ned apologized to Lonah and thanked him for saving his life.

Lonah continued. "Ned, I have a plan. We will return to Megadon for assistance, so let's get going. I'll tell you all about it on the way."

As Ned and Lonah began their return to Megadon, Ned's thoughts turned to the beautiful eyes of the dolphin he loved so dearly. He felt great remorse that he had failed her and the others.

Lonah sensed Ned's mood and now realized the wisdom of Megadon about how love could blind you and make you take risks. Ned had almost given up his life and the hopes of the ocean world to save Eccoh. This was admirable but not wise, Lonah realized. He grabbed the listless Ned up in his powerful mouth once again and swam swiftly for the rest of the morning. Ned was exhausted and gladly accepted the ride.

Ned and Lonah stopped to rest. Ned was refreshed now and able to continue on his own. Lonah began to tell Ned of his plan to rescue their friends. Ned listened wide eyed at the genius of Lonah's plan. His faith restored, he swam at Lonah's side as they set off once again to find Megadon.

Three Giant Worms were linked as one to keep the captured whales pinned to the sandy bottom. The heads of the other worms moved freely to keep lookout for the return of Ned or other potential rescuers. There was a hypnotic rhythm to their synchronized search pattern, swinging their heads from side to side. They appeared as harmless weeds, riding the movements of tide and current, and most likely many a hapless fish fell prey to this sea dance.

Kila turned to Flop, saying he felt betrayed. He also intimated that he was certain Ned and Lonah were instrumental in Kratch's plan to destroy the ocean paradise. He went on about Lonah being an agent for Kratch just as other sharks had been in the past.

Eccoh yelled at Kila to stop such ridiculous talk. She assured them that Ned and Lonah would return for them and would triumph over the Giant worms.

At that moment Zid popped his ugly head just outside the burrow next to Eccoh. "That's exactly what we hope they will do," he told the horrified captives. "And we hope this time to make them permanent guests, and seize the Map of Currents." Zid laughed ghoulishly.

Eccoh, Kila, and Flop felt their hopes sink as they realized that they were the bait to trap their friends.

Ned and Lonah arrived back at the very place the odyssey had begun. Megadon was visibly upset as he watched them approach. He swam hurriedly to meet them, and directed them to his favorite ledge. Ned and Lonah shared the story of the capture with Megadon and assured him all would be well, as they had a plan.

Before Megadon could respond, Ned asked if the Blue Whale had been eaten yet. Megadon replied that it hadn't, and would be weeks before it was.

Lonah and Ned exchanged glances. "Lord Megadon," Ned asked. "What would it take to devour the rest of that whale before the next light?"

Megadon was puzzled by the question, but answered without hesitation. "The Great Whites of my kingdom would have to allow all the other shark species to this sacred feast. It has never been allowed!"

Lonah and Ned explained the details of Lonah's plan as Megadon listened with great interest.

When Lonah finished, he immediately called for his most trusted lieutenant. Megadon was animated as he spoke about the new mission at hand. His lieutenant scurried off to implement Megadon's orders.

Megadon turned back to Lonah. "There will be thousands of sharks here in the next few hours," he said. "The Blue Whale will be clean to the bone by morning, as you requested.

Chapter Seven
A BLUE WHALE'S LAST MISSION

Imprisoned in the dark maze of caves, Naw lay sleeping. Since his capture, he had been shut off from all light, and his only visitor had been the gloating Kratch, bringing just enough food to keep him alive. In his depression and despair Naw spent increasing amounts of time in a state of sleep. It was in this state that his mind and spirit were able to, at times, communicate with Megadon.

Kratch burst into Naw's dark prison waking him. "Naw," he said. "Your great and wise father has outdone himself this time! We have already captured three of his so-called 'Warriors of Light', and soon we will have the others in our keeping as well. Megadon is becoming quite mad in his old age, sending such an inept group to face my challenge." He laughed again and watched Naw closely for his reaction.

Naw stayed composed and dignified. "My father," said Naw, "has always defeated you, regardless of the odds. He will do so again! Megadon will crush you, Lord of Darkness, when you least expect it!"

A shudder went through Kratch as he realized the truth of Naw's statement, but still managed an evil laugh as he left Naw to ponder the latest round of bad news.

Back on board the *Krill*, a choppy sea caused constant spray to wash over the windows of the pilothouse. The relentless pace of travel to get to the whaling grounds had taken its toll on the two professors. Conway finally convinced Miller to stop and heave-to for the night so they could get some sleep.

Before settling in, Miller sighted the whale that he had tagged weeks before. It was accompanying a cow and her calf on the migration south. He remembered the day he first tagged the whale but it also reminded him of the day he belittled his son in front of all his students. That insulting moment, he concluded, had set Ned to sulk at the stern and possibly sent him to his death. The next morning would put the *Krill* within two days of the whaling grounds, and Miller hoped the strange bird's prediction about Ned being there were correct. The professor bowed his head in silent prayer for his son and retired to his bunk.

In the cave of the Millennium Angel, things were getting worse. Her spirit was slowly fading, as were the prospects of her mission becoming a reality. Outside the cave the Bullycudas kept a constant watch, for no one was going to rescue the Angel without an all out battle.

Kila was rolled into a sandy pit shivering with fear as the Giant Worms held them captive. Eccoh and Flop were equally frightened. Kila and Flop exchanged harsh words about the poor planning and the obviously poor outturn.

"Kila," Flop said. "It does you no good to struggle with thoughts of Ned or Lonah being traitors or members of Kratch's evil plan. Time will answer any doubts very soon."

Eccoh confirmed her beliefs that the others would come to the rescue, but the two of them had better hurry, she said, as the worms seemed hungry and anxious to make a meal of them. She fought back tears as she, too, had pangs of doubt as to her fate in such a difficult situation.

"How can Ned and Lonah ever combat this many worms and win?" she thought.

Never before had Megadon allowed any deviation in the ritual feast of the whales, but Lonah's plan presented too great an opportunity to miss. Throughout the afternoon, and into the night, the waters around Megadon's domicile filled with the largest gathering of sharks ever seen. Hammerheads, Great Whites, Mako's and Black Tipped sharks arrived after being summoned by King Megadon. Surely this was the greatest force ever assembled.

As night wore on, Megadon left the frenzy, his mind reaching out to connect with Naw. Resting and concentrating, he immediately felt connected to the sleeping Naw. Each one drew love from the other as the hours of darkness enveloped them.

As morning came at last, Ned and Lonah approached Megadon. "All of these sharks are at your disposal," declared Megadon. "My son has given us his blessings for our plan. Surely our actions will spark outrage and a need for revenge from Kratch. We will deal with that as it comes."

After a sleepless night, Lonah and Ned eagerly met the dawn. Together they prepared to inspect the remains of the Blue Whale, where they found its bones stripped clean of flesh, while the ribs looked as if they had been sanded. Directly behind Ned were over a thousand sharks that had stayed to await their orders.

Ned turned to them and spoke. "Lonah will explain to all of you the brilliant plan he has devised to rescue our friends, and help resume our mission."

Lonah hesitated. He was not sure that this large gathering of sharks was prepared to take direction from him.

Megadon moved to his side and gave him a look of encouragement.

Lonah explained the plan and proceeded to direct the sharks in the process of dismantling the whale. Teams of great Whites gathered along each rib of the whale. Grasping a rib in their massive jaws, each team of seven sharks broke the rib free from the backbone of the whale. When the task was completed, the bones were arranged beside the whale in perfect order.

Ned took over then, and assigned teams of sharks to gather around the long, thick bones. He gave the command to lift and begin to move in formation toward the Burrows of the Giant Worms.

The bones were lifted and carried by rows of sharks positioned on either side, using their flippers as forklift tongs to support the weight from below. Thus, they carried their cumbersome cargo. As Ned watched the silent armada of bone-carrying sharks, he sent a prayer of gratitude to the spirit of the whale and to the All Knowing for their help.

Ned and Lonah moved to lead positions in the odd procession of the bones and the sharks, assuming the responsibility of leadership. Ned couldn't help but think that the scene he stared back at was similar to seeing an aircraft carrier. The mass of gray bodied sharks and the white of bone created a surrealistic backdrop. Ned and Lonah began to feel the immense responsibility of commanding such an ambitious attack on the Giant Worms, but he sheer power of numbers gave them confidence.

As they neared the upwelling area where Kila, Flop and Eccoh were captured, the tension mounted. At long last the menacing Giant Worms were to meet their match.

Before they reached the worms, a lone Bullycuda witnessed the departure of the Shark army. He hid behind a great rock until they passed and then made haste for Kratch. He wanted to alert the Giant Worms but there was no way to get around the sharks without detection. He decided there was only one option; tell Kratch as fast as he could!

When the messenger arrived and informed Kratch, there was a flurry of activity as General Slash assembled his troops to head out and assist the Giant Worms. More importantly to Kratch was the capture of the Warriors of Light. Bullycudas by the thousands began to descend on to the Burrows of the Giant Worms, preparing for battle.

Ned and Lonah halted the procession of sharks to let them rest for a few minutes and to prepare everyone for their assault on the worms. Ned reviewed their strategy and signaled the army to proceed. The sharks carrying the bones muscled up one last time, shoring and securing the long thick bones. The sharks then moved away from Ned and Lonah, leaving them alone at the bottom of the valley where they once slept under the spell of the Jellyfish Wizard. Lonah and Ned's eyes met, exchanging looks of encouragement and resolution. Quickly they began their ascent over the mineral encrusted hill.

The Giant Worms thrashed with menace as Lonah and Ned approached. Mock jabs of attack followed wild twists and turns with hissing and a look of terror from their bulging eyes. This was the welcome mat for Ned and Lonah.

Eccoh called out to Kila and Flop when she spotted the rescuers. The worm's knots binding them tightened as the rescuers came into view, but with just two opponents, the Giant Worms were confident of their victory.

Ned and Lonah edged slowly forward, and this angered the worms, impatiently waiting for their next victims. The worms assumed the pair were scared and were tempted to leave their burrows to chase after these foolish one's. Ned and Lonah were very close to the burrow where Zid had been hiding. Suddenly, Ned and Lonah began to retreat, spinning their bodies as a signal for the sharks to attack. The Giant Worms were totally unprepared.

Before the worms could react, the bones that were carried by the sharks were rammed into the open burrows. This effectively cut off any escape route for the Giant Worms. As each rib bone was pushed in more deeply, the Worms were forced from the protection of their burrows. Zid was nowhere in sight.

The Giant Worms panicked as they were driven from their holes and eaten by the swarming sharks. The knots that tied their captives were the first to be ripped to shreds by the voracious attackers. Kila came first to be with Ned and Lonah, followed by a relieved Flop. The turbulence from the battle churned the sandy bottom and obscured much of the activity.

Just as Ned spotted Eccoh coming his way, Zid's head emerged from the only remaining open holes and dragged Eccoh down into the burrow with him. Once again, Lonah restrained Ned. He made Ned wait until the sharks had eliminated all of the Giant Worms.

As the sand and silt began to settle, the sharks began schooling, searching for the last two Worms: Zid and his Queen. Ned yelled out to the sharks that Zid took Eccoh. Hearing this the sharks surveyed the burrows, listening for the slightest sounds of a struggle. An eerie silence began to terrify Ned.

Lonah perched over the buried bones and observed that

that there was a near perfect circle formed by the ribs of the Blue Whale. A discernible pattern emerged and Lonah could see that there was only one hole left unfilled. The problem was, there were no bones left to fill it. Freeing even a single bone from the burrows would take more time than Eccoh most likely had, deduced Ned. Without another whalebone left, Ned realized Zid and his queen had Eccoh and that revenge and hunger were both good reasons to believe she didn't have but a few more moments left to live.

From out of nowhere, the sharks looked on in amazement as an imposing image appeared in the distance. A massive gray white force was approaching at great speed. It was Megadon, and in his mouth was the huge skull of the Blue Whale. As Megadon neared the burrows, they directed him to the last open hole. He drove the head of the Blue Whale into the burrow with great force. The head closed and filled the hole and the earth around it erupted in an explosive thud. A tortured cry of agony came from beneath. The whole skull had injured either Zid or his Queen or both.

Both of them made a desperate attempt to flee through the final burrow on the other end of their private tunnel. Zid and his Queen emerged from the burrows simultaneously as Megadon engulfed Zid in an open sweep of his mouth. A wall of sharks quickly felled the Queen, ending her terrible reign. With a last wiggle of life, Zid's tail swayed hard to one side of Megadon's mouth. But with a final thrash of Megadon's head. Zid was gone. The death of the queen effectively ended the powerful alliance with the evil of the oceans.

Ned swam in desperate circles seeking any sign of Eccoh. Thoughts of Zid's revenge conjured ugly scenarios for he and his worried friends. Just then, a coughing sound came from beneath the sand. Scrambling to find the noise, Flop stirred the sand with his great flippers and uncovered the frightened and shaken Eccoh. In a tear-filled moment, the Warriors of Light were reunited.

Their reunion was interrupted by sharks, chanting: "Lonah ... Lonah ... Lonah!"

Lonah left his friends to swim amongst the sharks; the very sharks that had at one time shunned him. As each passed him, it bowed its head in salute to honor this toothless one whose brilliant plan led to the defeat of Zid and the menace of the Giant Worms.

The celebration was short lived. In the distance, the buzz of hundreds of oncoming Bullycudas was heard. The sharks readied for another battle as Megadon urged them to retreat. Megadon directed the sharks to lead the Bullycudas away from Ned and the Warriors of Light. The sharks, led by Megadon, swam in the direction of the oncoming Bullycudas. When they got close, they intended to outrun them in the direction opposite of the one Ned and the others had taken. Megadon's last command to the sharks was to create the necessary diversion, outdistance and escape the Bullycudas, and avoid battle. And they did!

Chapter Eight

THE CANYONS OF PERPETUAL DARKNESS

Ned, Kila, Flop, Eccoh and Lonah slipped again over the upwelling area, and at Flop's insistence, they joined forces to look for food. The hungry shark and his whale and dolphin friends were once again ready to develop their bubble feeding skills. Again, Flop was the star in the art of corralling fish. This time, even Kila willingly chased after the fish that were encircled by the walls of bubbles.

Lonah went off on his own, still feeling like a hero. He knew his father would hear of the tribute given to him by the other sharks and be proud of him at last. Eccoh began to seek out fish on her own. Outside the massive bubble clouds, she sensed, as did the others, a new independence and confidence.

As they fed, blinding rays of light penetrated the busy area where all of them were eating fish. This scepter of light was inviting them to discover its source. When they neared the surface, Eccoh gleefully announced that it was Dawinn, the mystical bird.

Ned was pleased at the prospect of seeing the strange bird again. Last time they met he had been drowning. This time he was safe and filled with an endless stream of questions. This bird was like no other, seeming to possess universal knowledge. Ned wondered if perhaps it was the All Knowing in the body of a bird.

As he surfaced and saw the beauty of the sky, Ned was moved to tears. He had been so captivated by the new underwater world, their quest, and his love for Eccoh, that he had forgotten about the wondrous beauty of the sky. The deep blues and puffy white clouds seemed foreign to him now. The thought that he might never return to land sent an unpleasant jolt through him.

Dawinn was waiting for them. This time the Bird seemed more luminous than before. The bands of gold and black were as Ned remembered, but now there was a bright egg-shaped halo around Dawinn as well. He didn't waste much time with the greeting of the five Warriors of Light as they surfaced. Eccoh was especially reverent of this messenger of the All Knowing. She breached at first sight of Dawinn, who recognized her gesture of respect for him and made his own aerial display as acknowledgment. His display was short, but impressive.

Dawinn began to address them. "I have troubling news concerning the Millennium Angel," he reported. "It appears her time here on Earth is being jeopardized by the lack of light in that horrendous prison Kratch has built around her. The All Knowing has instructed me to make you aware of the urgency of her rescue and to destroy Kratch. The Millennium Angel will perish without fulfilling her mission to return the world to a state of kindness," Dawinn finished.

"If we do not find the Tooth is there another way we can eliminate Kratch?" Eccoh asked Dawinn.

"No," Dawinn replied "There will be only one chance to wipe out this tyrannous master of evil. That is with the Tooth. You and the others are our only hope!

"The Map Of Currents is about to lead you to the Canyons Of Perpetual Darkness, is that correct?" asked Dawinn.

Ned unfurled the map to consult it and observed that they could be there by the next morning if they began the swim right away. Ned looked up at the nearly full moon appearing in the daylight hours. It was a sight he hadn't seen in a very long time.

"Dawinn," asked Ned. "Will this moon be full soon?"

Dawinn answered that the moon would be full the next day.

Ned had a strange look as he recalled what his father had told him about the full moon at this time of the year and it's strange effect on certain forms of sea life. Ned became giddy and began to laugh. To the others it seemed that such silly behavior was one of the human things Ned still did. Little did they know of the next brilliant plan he had conceived to foil Kratch!

"I have one more question I'd like to ask you Dawinn, if you don't mind," said Ned.

"Yes, but be brief, as your hours are numbered, and the Millennium Angel is desperately close to dying," Dawinn reminded him.

"Yes, of course you're right Dawinn. Just tell me if the corals on this map are alive or dead."

Dawinn looked at the Map of Currents and replied that the coral reefs were very much alive. There was sufficient filtered light for the coral to continue to thrive.

"As a matter of fact," Dawinn told them, "this is where Kratch gathered the very coral to entomb the Millennium Angel.

"Remember this," he advised. "Kratch and his Bullycudas hate the light and the Canyons of Perpetual Darkness are their favorite hideout because of this. They know these dark canyons well, Ned, and this will be the most dangerous time of your lives. By now Kratch is well aware of your conquest of Zid and the Giant Worms. He has enlisted the aid of any available ally to make sure you never leave the Canyons of Perpetual Darkness with the Tooth."

Ned smiled as he stared at the moon and then looked back at the map. He seemed lost in the moment, oblivious to what Dawinn had just told them. "What? What are you staring at?" he said, when he saw the strange look they were giving him.

Dawinn interrupted by circling them with a ball of light that lingered over them. "Let the light be your answer to all of the problems in the Canyons of Perpetual Darkness," were his words as he disappeared. They all watched as Dawinn's glow of yellow light exploded and faded into nothingness.

Ned gathered them to hear the new plan for the canyons and Kratch. He told of how the full moon would alter the activity in the canyons and exactly how he thought they could slip by unnoticed by any Bullycudas, or even Kratch. He told them of the bloom of the coral reefs and the mating season of many fish that coincided with the arrival of the full moon. This moon would light the waters like no other time of year, and he silently prayed that Kratch was unaware of this unique scenario.

The warriors listened intently. "Time will judge our success. Now, let's be off to the canyons!" The Warriors of Light swam into a golden sunset to test fate once again.

Kratch and General Slash were on the outer fringes of the Canyons Of Perpetual Darkness discussing how they might capture the Warriors of Light. General Slash indicated to the Bullycudas, who had returned without success in finding Ned or engaging the sharks in battle, should continue searching for the Tooth. Slash and Kratch would patrol the entire region of the Canyons for the anticipated guests.

Kratch knew that time was running out for the Warriors of Light to complete their mission. He also knew that after their victory at the Burrows of the Giant Worms, they might be feeling over confident. He hoped that by the second dawning of day they would see the five Warriors of Light swimming directly into his evil path. Kratch turned to General Slash and told him to capture the Map, Ned, and the others. Death would be the price of failure, a slow and painful death.

With his life at stake, General Slash was highly motivated to succeed.

Ned explained to his friends that each full moon generates changes in the energy fields all over the world. However, this particular full moon's energy has a different effect on certain animals and plants. The coral worlds, during this time of year, experience their annual bloom. The coral, which are animals, release multicolored clouds of spores into the sea. Spouting from the coral heads, the spores get carried away in the ocean currents to form colonies hundreds of miles away.

Ned's friends listened intently but couldn't understand how this information could be useful to them.

Finally, Eccoh interrupted Ned in mid sentence. "What does all this information about coral spores, or *anything* about coral have to do with our mission?"

Ned chuckled to himself as he realized that he sounded just like his father. "First," he replied, "this is the only time of year that these coral release their colorful clouds of spores. Secondly, it's the only time of year when the reefs that lead to the Canyons Of Perpetual Darkness are light enough for us to find our way to where Naw dropped the Tooth. Finally, it is a time of year when hundreds of species of fish congregate to mate, eat and witness this miracle of nature.

"When the tide is high, at the full moon, the water is totally still, the temperature rises and a chemical effect produces a reaction that triggers the release of the coral spores like a million flowers that bloom at an instant. It will be a collage of color and movement that brings fish, like the male and female Parrot fish, to fertilize eggs.

"These eggs mix with, and float to safety camouflaged by the coral spores. This attracts millions of smaller fish that will feast on the coral spores and the fertilized eggs of the Parrot fish. Thousands of barracuda and sharks also arrive to join the colorful festivities, all of which will divert the attention of the Bullycudas as we travel along to the bottom of the reef just below all the activity. As the full moon sparks fireworks of spores illuminating the entire area, some light will penetrate to the depth of the coral reef. Below, the light will be limited to a few hours.

"So you see, we must get beyond the reef to the darkest part of the canyons before the light fades. That's where we'll find the Tooth. We all know that Kratch cannot tolerate any light without great pain to his eyes, so he won't be anywhere near the reef." Ned finished with a big smile.

Kila asked the next question. "How will this make any difference once we are beyond the reef?"

Ned hesitated and simply told them the truth. "I don't know, Kila. At that point we'll need a miracle."

"When do we head for the Canyons?" asked an enthusiastic Lonah.

"We will have to wait one more day as the moon is not quite full," Ned informed them. "This means we'll arrive on the eve of the full moon."

"What do we do in the meantime?" asked Flop.

"We eat, Flop," Ned replied with a smile. "We just eat and rest."

This was a very satisfactory answer, and everyone, including Kila, began to pursue the nearest school of fish.

The canyons were full of the bustling and anxious Bullycudas. Teams of Kratch's silvery followers darted from place to place looking for the Warriors of Light. The hunt was intense and competitive. The Bullycuda that would catch Ned and the others would have status, and a level of power equal to that currently held by Slash.

Tensions were thick with fear and anticipation by Kratch's soldiers, and especially Slash, who feared for his life if they failed. They would all have to wait for the full moon before any high adventure would play out. Besides, the expected guests were filling up on schooling fish.

The Map Of Currents showed that the coral reefs created very deep walls that dropped from sight in the Canyons of Perpetual Darkness. Over many thousands of years, the live coral grew to great heights reaching toward the sunlight. In those depths there were many layers of dead coral and limestone deposits. This created the foundation for the live coral, and was where the Warriors would hide. The time was nearing for the Warriors of Light to make their way to the edge of the reef and then to the deepest ravines of the canyons.

It was time for Ned and the Warriors to make their way

to the coral reefs. As they swam toward the reef they saw many sharks and barracudas. They were ignored by all of these predators so intent on reaching the reefs.

"Perhaps the primordial need to participate in this full moon event is everything Ned claimed," thought Kila, feeling somewhat relieved.

Hammerheads, Tiger, and Nurse sharks passed overhead. The route to the reefs had suddenly become an easy path for the Warriors of Light. They joined the thousands of animals that now formed a procession to one of nature's most colorful displays. Ned remembered his father telling him that the astronauts had seen it from the moon, it was so bright.

"Does Kratch know?" wondered Ned. "And, if he does, what would his strategy be to catch them?" This nagging thought pursued him.

The moon neared full, and the temperature of the water changed noticeably. The travelers were nervous with anticipation. The reefs were still a blur in the distance as sharks swam in figure eight's, looping around barracudas schooling within feet of them. There was no hunting, no feeding — they all waited expectantly. The fireworks of spores from the coral would be the signal that would ignite a frenzy of activity.

Ned, Eccoh, Flop, Lonah and Kila worked their way to the bottom edge of the first reef. There they paused just below the vigorous activity. The arrival of Bullycudas suddenly added new tension to the environment of lust filled Parrot fish, as they were opportunistic feeders, and would be heroes in searching for the Tooth.

The Bullycudas arrival was timely since the warriors had just managed to snuggle into shelter below the coral when they passed by. This very deep and wide crevice hid a large Moray Eel. Lonah had been brave enough to scare it off temporarily.

Ned was certain that the Bullycudas would return. Eccoh kept a watch for the possibility and continued to peek just outside the crystallized rock. Suddenly she noticed Kila's dorsal fin was protruding one foot above an opening in the rock. She could also see that the Bullycudas were returning to search this area again. She froze in place, realizing that any sudden movement by her would create turbulence in the water, exposing them all. The tide was totally still. The water temperature was warm and the moon was now full. It seemed to Eccoh that the Bullycudas would spot them any moment.

Miraculously, it all began.

The spores of the coral spewed clouds of pink, red, and orange that mixed with smaller clouds of purple and blue greens and the ocean lit up! The approaching Bullycudas could not resist the primal urge to feed upon the bounty of fish before them. This was the ocean's quintessential light show and drama of life and death.

Now the Warriors carefully swam to the corals open edge where the canyon met the deep recesses of accumulated limestone. What they saw there was amazing! Miles of of reef festooned with brightly colored bundles of spores and rainbows of spouting coral. Spores floated to the surface, magically dissolving, while releasing the two essential players of life, the sperm and the egg. In the brilliant moonlit waters these life forms floated, seeking each other and merging with love to create their future.

Ned figured there would be enough time for them to get by the reef and enter the deepest confines of the canyons to search for the Tooth. No doubt, in the deepest and darkest, they would find Kratch or he would find them.

The Bullycudas believed they would find Ned and his cohorts amongst the clouds of spores. This camouflage would only work for a few hours, so the Bullycudas felt confident that they would pick them out and capture them. The millions of spores looked like a bouquet of flowers that stretched for miles.

Kila, Flop, Lonah, Eccoh and Ned swam at a steady pace, still able to witness the remarkable feeding frenzy of the tiny fish that gulped thousands of eggs from the illuminated waters. Rows of fan coral swayed loosely in the warm waters, as the pause at high tide gave way to the tug of the receding tide. The low tide's essential role of sweeping the united coral spores out into the open ocean was underway.

Ned and the others were now comfortably away from the Bullycudas and had made their way beyond the reefs undetected. As they approached the entrance to the canyons, Ned spotted some seals involved in a game of chase, similar to the one Kila, Eccoh and Flop had played back at the Ocean Haven. The seals chased a small school of fish over the reef and into the canyons. Ned watched as they disappeared into the canyon's deep abyss. Suddenly, they were in sight again, despite the darkness of the waters. They were spinning in circles around the fish, challenging them to escape. It was only a game for the seals, but to Ned, this sight was the answer to a prayer.

Ned approached the seals slowly, and as he neared, their twisting ballet came to a halt. The leader of the seals, a large male, put himself between Ned and his group of seals. Flop edged closer to them to give a friendly greeting. He told the bull seal that he was safe, and that the five creatures he saw were on a special mission for Megadon and the Ocean of Light.

This information seemed to calm the seals, and Ned was impressed by the majesty of the wide-eyed, brown skinned, three hundred pound seal leader. A bright orange gold patch above his eye set him apart from the others. Ned quickly told them of their mission and the plans they had.

"Have you ever been to the deeper portions of this canyon?" he asked the seal.

The seal replied that this is where they found many of their favorite foods such as starfish, crabs and snails.

"How do you find it in the darkness," asked Ned.

"It's simple," informed the bull seal. "We create our own light."

"By spinning in circles, you light up the bottom. Correct?"

"Yes, the bottom is very dark," said the bull seal. "But the plants that float give us temporarily light. You can create light anywhere, anytime. We have learned to make the light our ally."

Ned went on to tell the seals that Kratch was undoubtedly down in the canyons and looking for he and his friends.

The bull seal nodded to the handful of others waiting nearby and without another word they all swam off. The Warriors thought this departure was very strange. Lonah had recognized the leader by it's orange marking. It was the seal he had refused to eat the day his father tested him in the open kelp beds. Now fate had brought them together again amid the Canyons of Perpetual Darkness.

"The way to find the Tooth is to create our own light," Ned told his nervous companions. "As we go through the canyons, we will spin as one and light up the way. Hopefully, we can find the Tooth before we encounter Kratch, General Slash, or the Bullycudas."

As they neared the place where Naw dropped the Tooth, Ned began the slow circling motion and signaled the others to follow his lead. Eccoh stayed close to Ned, Lonah was in the middle of this cyclone action, and Flop chose to stay behind Kila, who was feeling faint with fear.

The plan seemed to be working: the light exposed

craggy edges of the canyon's walls. Once under this shelf of rock, it became darker still and more frightening as they spun while searching on. At the greater depths, the spinning was less effective and they went for long periods when no light was generated. They were only able to sense each other's movement in the waters, but in this way managed to stay together.

Suddenly, Eccoh saw a flicker of white extending from the sand; pointed and smooth, with a smattering of barnacles. It was the Tooth. Before Eccoh could utter a word, huge eyes approached them. Kratch had finally found these upstarts and swam toward them slowly, enjoying the state of shock and horror they were feeling.

Eccoh urged them to spin and create light, but it was useless, they were mesmerized by the bulging eyes of Kratch and the fear that held them frozen in its grip. The sparkle of General Slash's scales flashed in the black waters as they inched closer.

From behind Kratch and Slash, Ned saw an approaching green neon ball of light. He thought it must be hundreds of Bullycudas coming to assist their leaders. They were doomed, and Ned and Eccoh touched flippers in a gesture of love. Lonah bravely edged ahead of the others so they could attempt escape. Flop encouraged Kila to swim away as fast as he could for with killer whale speed. At least he had a chance.

Kratch was now close enough that they could see his purplish blood shot eyes and his massive gray body. Lonah was planning to ram Kratch as soon as he came another foot closer. The General was now also visible, his jaws quivering in anticipation. The neon ball of light was closing in rapidly, and Kratch and General Slash turned simultaneously to see the arrival.

In an instant, this oncoming cyclone of light was over Kratch and Slash like the swarming bees. It was the seals!

Hundreds of seals circled and blinded Kratch. He slashed with his razor sharp fin's hoping to strike these brazen seals. He did manage to wound one slightly but the seals were too quick for him and he was helpless in his blindness. Kratch closed his eyes to block the light.

Lonah grabbed Slash by the lower half of his body and pulled and thrashed him into submission. The waters lit up with the seal's relentless circling of Kratch, and an occasional swipe with his fin's was all he could manage to fend off the seals. The light painfully penetrated his sensitive, though closed eyes.

Ned looked up to see Eccoh swimming toward him. His eyes lit up in astonishment when he saw that she was holding the key to their success: the Tooth! Eccoh had sighted the Tooth and grabbed it during Kratch's slow approach. Next, Flop swam over to join them, as did a badly shaken Kila. Lonah was still dragging the frustrated General away from his helpless leader. Lonah's grip on the lower half of the General's body cut off the blood supply and crippled him long enough to enable him to join his friends.

When Lonah saw them and the Tooth held by Eccoh, his heart was filled with joy. Ned quickly pieced together a ragged, but sturdy pouch of seaweeds to hold the Tooth and Eccoh proudly placed it inside for Ned.

The orange-patched bull seal broke from the raiding circle and urged Ned and the others to leave quickly. Ned asked the seal how they found them in such dark waters.

"A wild-eyed Jellyfish Wizard lighted our way to you," the seal told Ned. "And then disappeared as soon as you were in sight."

"It's impossible," Ned exclaimed. "That Jellyfish has been an enemy of this mission from the start!"

"Believe whatever you may Ned," the seal said emphatically. "But the jellyfish is the only reason you are here to ask me any questions. Go now or Kratch will catch us all!"

A second bull seal was dispatched to lead them out of the Canyons of Perpetual Darkness. They had won again. Kratch was still besieged by seals, but General Slash was coming to. It was time to go. Bullycudas still searched for them high above in the reefs among the hundreds of Parrot fish, sharks and whales. The colorful celebration of coral spores was even more of a celebration than ever before. Ned, Eccoh, Kila, Flop and Lonah followed their new friend away from danger.

Ned couldn't help but swim off thinking of the series of odd actions the Jellyfish Wizard had taken in this journey. He dropped the Tooth in the presence of Snap, then led the charge of the seals directly to Kratch. Were these the actions of an evil Wizard, or had they somehow gained an ally? Ned thought back to the Giant Worms and how the Wizard's used tricks to entrap them.

One thing was certain: the Jellyfish Wizard was a mystery!

Chapter Nine

IN ARMS WAY

The *Krill* swayed from side to side as Professors Conway and Miller stirred in their bunks. The long journey had taken its toll on the two men, and they slept on board in four hour shifts. Professor Conway awoke first, making coffee and wearily checking the *Krill* for any leaks. There were none. As Professor Miller continued to rest between sleep and consciousness, Conway unlocked a cabinet in which he had been hiding a surprise for his friend.

He pulled out a file containing notes and scrolls of paper from the boat's hydrophone recorder and he set them down on the dinette in the galley. Soon the smell of fresh coffee would call the sleeping professor to wakefulness.

"Good morning," Conway said to his half awake colleague.

"Good morning to you my friend," Miller replied.

"I'd better pour a big cup for you today because I have the results of your radio tag here on the desk," Conway informed the pleased and surprised professor. "While you slept, I ran the recorder and hydrophone overboard. It took a day of travel, but I picked up a signal and have successfully tracked our whale ever since. When we find

Ned and return to the lab we can analyze the data and determine the validity of your migration theory. We're only one day from the whaling grounds, so let's get there and find Ned."

Miller was moved by his friend's surprise and for a brief moment the loss of Ned slipped his tortured mind.

In the depths of the ocean, Naw slept deeply in his dark, lonely prison. Megadon again appeared in his dreams. This time the dream was of a swim his father was making to the coast where the spirits of sharks are separated from their physical bodies. In this most mystical place, where the shoreline met the ocean, was revealed a resting place for weary, old sharks that wished to free their spirits to the love of the All Knowing. Megadon and Naw swam the final miles together while Megadon reflected on the Kingdom of Light and the immense responsibility that being its leader had entailed.

Naw awoke from his dream realizing that this was prophetic, for in the past, they had always come true. He was sure he would see his father again, and felt his spirits lift as he let this truth sink in.

In another part of the sea, Ned, the bull seal and the triumphant Warriors of Light were now safely out of the Canyons of Perpetual Darkness. They realized that the previous episode with Kratch would not be their last, and that the final leg of the Map of Currents would at some point involve a showdown. The bull seal had been incredibly helpful in getting them back on track. Having once encountered Kratch, none of them were eager to meet him again, though they knew they must.

The bull seal explained why their leader had left so suddenly. "All of our seals have an independence that is essential to our survival, and the decision to assist you in your quest was made by each seal. When we heard of your plight, there were many more volunteers than you saw. It was determined that only half of us would be needed to ensure your success, and we were right.

"Our leader wasn't being rude to you," he explained, bidding farewell. "Only exercising the code we live by."

Kila swam along with him for a while in a gesture of gratitude and eventually turned back to join the others.

Ned unfurled the Map of Currents one last time. They were amazed at how much territory they had covered. They all took a moment to absorb the significance of their success and accomplishments with the exception of Kila. He was still dreaming of his ledge in the Haven. Flop and Lonah studied the map and thought about how clever Kratch had been in calculating the obstacles of anyone who accepted his challenge. He knew that the map would eventually lead to the depths of his dark world and the traps laid there.

What Kratch hadn't predicted was the ingenuity and courage of the latest challengers. Naw was an example of a powerful being that underestimated the dangers of the currents and fell into Kratch's trap.

The next danger facing them was in passing through the domain of Tentacle. Megadon had warned them that Tentacle was a tricky and hostile creature. Ned believed that they could easily swim past the territory.

He was wrong.

Kratch was enraged that Ned and the Warriors of Light were nearing their goal. For the first time, he began to experience anxiety and doubt about the outcome. He comforted himself with the thought that they would not know where to place the Tooth when the time came for the warriors to do so. Only he and the General were privy to that information. Their time was running out, and if Ned or one of his comrades failed to lodge the Tooth in the proper place before sunrise the next day, he would reign victorious. The world would belong to him fair and square.

General Slash still lay bleeding only a hundred yards from Kratch. Rather than kill him for failing to stop the intruders of the Canyons of Perpetual Darkness, he had decided to let him suffer a long, slow death on the dark ocean bottom. He would be an example to the others. The Bullycudas were ashamed they had let the General down and they were forced to watch as Kratch belittled, then injure their once great general with his razor sharp flipper.

Kratch signaled the move to the final showdown with Ned and the Warriors of Light. The Bullycudas were ordered to proceed to the cave of the Millennium Angel to ward off Megadon's Great White Sharks. Kratch led the army of Bullycudas — a dispirited and reluctant army.

A handful of loyal and concerned soldiers stayed behind to see if they could save the injured leader. They knew this decision to disobey Kratch could also cost them their lives, but they had to try. The General's situation was grim, his wounds were deep and life threatening.

Water temperatures were rising as Ned, Lonah, Kila, Flop and Eccoh began the final leg of their journey. Hundreds of Man o' War's drifted by, their neon blue and long red tentacles trailing like streamers in a watery parade. Colored fish added to the mix of abundant life forms present. Ned realized that they were very close to the whaling grounds. These fish species were not ones the whales would eat. In these waters, the whales rarely fed as winter approached. Tending newborn calves and mating were the business of the whales that migrated to this part of the ocean.

The influx of large numbers of animals made the hunting of whales easy here. Through instinct, not choice, the whales returned to these same places throughout their lives. The pattern supported their cycles of reproduction, yet simultaneously placed them in great peril.

Ned tried to maintain his vigilance and resisted the temptation of being distracted by the peaceful environment.

Kila and Flop suddenly picked up a distress call, and the sounds became audible even to Ned and Lonah. Soon desperate cries filled the waters. A mother whale was calling to her calf to be brave, telling it she was on her way. Eccoh was informed of what was happening since she could not echo locate or understand the sounds.

Flop explained to the others what was happening. "Tentacle has her calf, and is using it as bait to capture and kill them both. This time even plants can't light up the waters. The blackness of Tentacle's traps is created by millions of small squid that eject ink whenever he demands they do so."

Flop caught the mother sperm whale before she was lured into Tentacle's trap. He warned her that she would soon be captive if she mindlessly swam to her calves' aid.

"Mother sperm," began Flop. "Your calf is only being held to lure you into Tentacle's trap. He has used this ploy successfully many times since a bull sperm whale ate his son. Tentacle wants revenge. He would love to torture you for hours with the calling of your calf. He will not harm the calf until you give in and charge blindly into his dark trap. Do you understand?"

She indicated her understanding and awaited Flop's instructions. All the Warriors of Light arrived and huddled together to assist in creating a plan to free the calf.

The cries from the calf continued. Ned feared that this further delay might prove fatal to the Millennium Angel and their mission. Without help, Tentacle could hold the calf for hours, even days. Ned knew they needed divine intervention here or they were going to fail.

He surfaced to seek a sign and noticed a number of

boats steaming by. One was rolling drift nets over its side. Ned recognized these nets from the many films his father had shown to educate students about these environmental nightmares. These nets snared everything in their paths and killed them. Ned shook his head in disgust and looked for any sign. There was none.

Sadly, Ned swam back to the panicked mother and his friends where he and they rejected a number of plans for the rescue of the calf. As the discussion continued, Ned noticed a number of small squid retreating into the murky darkness. Ned and Lonah swam to the bottom to investigate while the others stayed to comfort the mother sperm.

At the bottom was an opening comprised of two steep, jagged ledges. Ned and Lonah perceived the ledges were at least forty five feet apart and created a natural gateway. Ned swam toward this rocky appendage in curiosity. Above them they heard the sounds of the motors of the drift net fishermen's boat.

As the boat slowed and stopped, Ned had an inspired thought. "Quick Lonah," he said. "Let's get back to the others as fast as we can."

They swam rapidly into the tight gathering of their friends, where Ned explained his plan. He explained how nets work and how they would have to take them from the fishermen at the surface.

Using Lonah as a decoy, Ned knew that the sight of a Great White Shark would totally distract the fishermen from their work. He was told to tease them, but not to open his toothless mouth. The fishermen would try to lure him near the boat and kill him if they could.

Eccoh suggested that they stage a mock battle between the whales and Great White at a safe distance from the boat. Ned told her it was a brilliant idea and to the humans, it would be irresistible. They would surely abandon all fishing to see such a spectacle in the open seas. While the mock battle was performed at the surface, Ned would attempt to cut and steal the net. His only remaining problem was how he could quickly cut through the brittle netting with only his teeth.

The mother sperm echoed back to her calf. What information she was able to convey to her calf must have been comforting for the calf stopped whimpering for the first time that day. She knew they were far from accomplishing a rescue, but she had great hope and faith in Ned and the others. The final elements of the plan were discussed and the time for action was at hand.

Tentacle was perplexed. None of his previous entrapments of calves had ever failed. All the other whales had rushed to the rescue at the slightest squeal of protest from their calves. The presence of these Warriors of Light had begun to make Tentacle nervous. The smaller squid kept Tentacle informed. They had seen Kila, who frightened them enough that they made an effort to keep a long distance from him.

Tentacle wasn't sure how to handle this now quiet calf and possibly disinterested mother. This wasn't supposed to happen. By now, he usually had the mother and calf in the grasp of his long tentacles. His thoughts turned to his son that had been killed so many years before. Since then, revenge had become his life's mission. He was an empty and miserable being, and the other squid pitied him — but they also feared his wrath.

The motors of the fishing vessel rumbled steadily at the surface. The starboard side of the boat began to fill with the excited yelling of sailors. A five foot dorsal had surfaced right along side of them. It was a Great White Shark!

The younger crew members were awe struck, and the older ones felt chills of fear. This shark was the nightmare of all sea going men. They chattered excitedly as Lonah made a close approach and then disappeared — only to appear again seconds later at the bow or stern; but always on the starboard side.

Ned and Eccoh had worked their way to the port side where the net lay over the side. They heard the crew explode with excitement as Kila and Flop joined in action. The crew leaned over the rigging waiting for the confrontation of predator and prey. Kila charged Lonah at high speed as Lonah, like a matador, swiveled away just as Kila was within inches of him. Frequent underwater dives prolonged the action and the sailors remained transfixed as the 'battle' unfolded before them. Ned spotted a fisherman's knife on the deck just below the scuppers, and when he heard the roar of the sailors, he made his move.

They were jeering and yelling like sports fans for their

favorite team. Flop lay on his side and flapped his huge flippers to fake the mock shark attack. Lonah came from below Flop's belly with Kila hot on his tail as Kila breached to add to the spectacle. Ned came up on his tail as he had seen in the aquariums and snagged at the knife. He missed. He tried again, but couldn't keep his balance long enough.

Eccoh could see what he was doing and expertly reached the knife. She grabbed it with her mouth and pushed it overboard with her flipper. Eccoh and Ned had talked out the rest of the daring act as they both sprang into action. Next, as they agreed, she grabbed the leading edge of the net that lay at the surface hanging from a fixed roller at the stern. She twisted and turned the net into a rope-like shape so Ned could cut it more efficiently.

The sailors were getting restless over the amount of time lost from their work, and some began to turn back to their duties. Lonah and Kila made another close approach to the boat to keep them engaged but to no avail. One of the crew noticed Ned and Eccoh cutting the net and alerted the others. They all scrambled to the starboard side as the captain picked up a harpoon and ran to the roller containing his net. Ned was almost finished.

The captain was furious, and his mates stood back to give him room with the harpoon. The captain was an experienced whaler and Ned and Eccoh presented an easy target for him. The two of them were easy prey for this killer of whales.

Ned refused to escape and continued to cut the net

despite the danger. Eccoh courageously held her ground, remaining at Ned's side.

The captain raised the harpoon, lifting slowly back over his heavily muscled right shoulder. As he began to throw the harpoon, a fifteen foot long flipper came up over the stern, sweeping the captain overboard.

Flop rolled on his side and slapped next to the captain with his enormous flipper. Then Lonah then made a pass within feet of the struggling captain, who was now in fear for his life. Lonah opened his mouth as he approached the terrified captain. As soon as the captain looked into the shark's toothless mouth, he realized they had been tricked.

In the midst of the chaos, Ned and Eccoh were able to cut the last fibers of the net and begin to pull it to the bottom. They had successfully retrieved the net and stopped the sailors above from committing the atrocity of drift netting.

The mother sperm whale had watched and prayed from afar. They had succeeded and were ready to undertake the next phase of their plan.

Kila reached safety first. He'd left before the others, and was ashamed of his cowardice. If there had been a sudden need for his help, he wouldn't have been there. He did participate in the mock attack on Lonah, but that was more of a game Kila played with Lonah and Flop.

Ned continued to be very concerned about the liability of Kila's fear. He assumed that when the time to confront Kratch arrived, Kila would not be available. He secretly wished Kila had gone back to the Ocean Haven when he'd had the chance.

The mother sperm joined the Warriors of Light surrounding the tangled net. Ned directed them as the joined forces to untangle and stretch the net out. They next swam to the gateway between the rocks that Ned had discovered and set the net. All but Kila gathered together as their planned rescue continued.

The next stage was set in motion as the mother Sperm Whale entered the murky, ink filled waters as if she were attempting a rescue. As she came close to Tentacle she turned back, and he released the calf to pursue her.

Ned and the others braced for the arrival of the two giants. Time dragged and minutes felt like hours. Suddenly, the sounds of two enormous creatures approaching them were heard. They held the net steady in the current and prayed that Tentacle would swim into it.

Tentacle lunged at the tail of the sperm and, as they came closer, strengthened his grip on her, and began to slow her down. Tentacle caught her a hundred yards from the trap. The plan was unraveling disastrously.

Ned ordered Flop, Eccoh and Lonah to free the net and cover the two beasts with it. Tentacle didn't see the net that covered him and the mother sperm until it was tightened, and prevented any movement from either. The two were trapped together with the mother sperm's teeth embedded in one of the many tentacles that surrounded her head and jaws. Without effect, Tentacle writhed in an attempt to free himself. Eventually they both tired. As their struggle ceased, Ned moved forward to free them from the Net.

"Tentacle, you are a clever and bold warrior," Ned said. "Your life has been one of great suffering over the loss of your son. The story is known the oceans over. Today, you have found yourself in a difficult place. We have ways to free the mother sperm and keep you in this net, and, if you wish to die here, you shall. I will give you the choice."

"What do you propose to do that would free me from this thing you call a net?" Tentacle asked.

"Well, to begin, if you agree to leave the whales alone while they migrate with their calves, and if this mother sperm agrees to let the whales know they aren't to bother you or your school of squid, I will cut you free."

"What makes you think that when you let me loose I won't kill all of you?" asked Tentacle.

"Trust," said Ned. "I will simply believe you, that's all."

Tentacle lowered his eyes and thought for a moment. "Cut me free, Ned," a stern but sincere Tentacle told the relieved Warrior of Light. "I will take this mother to her calf."

The net was torn to pieces with the knife and the teeth of Kila, Eccoh, and the mother sperm. When they were untangled, Tentacle stretched his arms and gave Ned a scary look that soon became a smile. It seemed that Tentacle had a sense of humor.

Ned and the others urgently needed to get to the final encounter with Kratch, and decided to leave Tentacle and the mother sperm to attend to her calf. But before they could leave, a school of squid rushed to Tentacle's side. They alerted him to the arrival of Slash and his escorts.

The Jellyfish Wizard accompanied the General. The inky waters were clearing and the Warriors of Light watched in amazement as the wounded general made his way to Ned. Slash's teeth still presented an imposing sight. For a moment Ned wondered if Tentacle would double cross him, considering he had his old allies present.

The Jellyfish Wizard spoke first. "Warriors of Light, you have overcome many obstacles and are close to defeating Kratch. The General and I come to offer you our services in the final encounter."

"The two of you have been against us from the beginning," Ned replied. "Why would you want to help us now, and why should we believe you?"

The Wizard and the general edged closer. "Come here Ned," said the Wizard softly. "Please don't fear me now. If I had wanted you to die, I would have carried you and Lonah off to the Burrows of the Giant Worms with the others."

"Yes," said Ned suspiciously. You could have easily done us all in. What are you up to, Wizard?"

Suddenly the Wizard spun wildly creating a whirlpool of water below him that looked like a crystal ball. In this whirlpool they could all see Kratch's hiding place and home. In it, three Jellyfish swam cautiously around the sleeping Naw.

"You see those three Jellyfish, Ned? They are my sons.

Kratch has held them hostage for some time. He knew that I would be forced to assist him whenever he asked to ensure their safety. He told me he would free my sons if I would help him kill the great Megadon. Kratch is a liar and as evil as one can get, so I would rather work with you to set my sons free. When Kratch is defeated, the general, the Bullycudas and I will help to free the Millennium Angel. Then I will go seek out Megadon and lead him to his son."

General Slash groaned in pain. The gash in his side was hideous, and he was held afloat by five comrades that risked their lives to help save him. General Slash looked thoughtfully at the warriors before he spoke. "I'll be brief," he started, "I know that you are leaving here to confront Kratch. I also know that, aside from the Map of Currents, Kratch had given you the task of finding the spot you are to target in order to kill him."

General Slash eyed the Tooth that Ned had secured to his side, then continued. "Kratch confided in me, and only me, where that spot is. After I finished confining the Angel, I was there with the Jellyfish Wizard when Kratch pulled the Tooth from the right side of his body, just below his flipper. He told us that Megadon missed by inches the very spot that would have been fatal to him."

The General pointed to Flop and placed his flipper under Flops'. "This is where you'll find his uncaring heart. You must place it there precisely to destroy him."

General Slash began to falter and Lonah swam to help him stay afloat. Tentacle moved in the circle of supporters as well, and at the same time ordered his smaller squid to leave and help the mother sperm.

Tentacle chose to come to Slash's aid. "The Wizard and I will care for the General from now on, Ned. But you had better go, or you will fail in your mission.

As the Warriors of Light turned to go, General Slash said: "Be sure you succeed."

The Warriors acknowledged him and wished him well.

When they had disappeared from sight, Tentacle, the Jellyfish Wizard and General Slash made a vow to swim to the cave of the Millennium Angel together and be the first to help free her.

The participants in this saga of good and evil were converging upon the whaling grounds where the final encounter would be played out.

Chapter Ten

SHOWDOWN WITH EVIL

Now that the mystery of where to put the Tooth had been solved, the Warriors of Light were more optimistic. But even so, the problem of who would place the Tooth into Kratch was still in question. Ned knew that none of the Warriors of Light had the power physically, nor the wits mentally to outsmart Kratch. They may have fooled him once, but this time he was would be prepared.

They were all fearful, and Kila found it hard to swim, so preoccupied was he with seeing Kratch again. It wasn't a long distance to the whaling grounds, but this stretch seemed the most difficult. The burden of their mission was weighing heavily on them as they approached the final encounter. Ned led them to the surface for one last rest.

As they surfaced, the sight of over a hundred spouts filled the horizon. Whales had been arriving at the winter grounds for days as they had for thousands of years. Some returned with the calf from the previous winter, others were arriving to deliver a newborn this season.

What a grand sight it was, in stark contrast was the sight of metal flashing from the opposite direction as the whaling boats arrived to slaughter the whales. The Warriors of Light came to eliminate Kratch, and soon the wee hours of morning would be upon them.

Ned gave the signal to move on, but before they

submerged, Dawinn flew in to greet them. As usual, his visit was a timely one. Ned needed some encouragement to steady him and Dawinn always seemed to bring renewed courage and strength with him.

Dawinn hovered over them in excitement. He said the oceans were abuzz with the tales of their victorious adventures. Megadon had asked Dawinn to send his highest regards to all of them, especially to Ned.

"Megadon wants you to know of the strong bond he feels for all of you," Dawinn went on. "He considers you his sons and daughters. Many creatures are praying for you and he wants you to draw from that energy when you confront Kratch in the morning."

Strong currents carried them along swiftly, and according to the map, when the pull or push of current ended, they would find themselves in the presence of Kratch. At times, the current allowed them to rest. Finally, they floated gently into the dreaded whaling grounds.

Schools of colorful fish passed them going against the current and Lonah explained why. "They are aware of an evil presence ahead," he warned. No further explanation was necessary. They had traveled through the night, and now a fuzzy gray morning permeated the water. They felt an eerie stillness in the current. It slowed and stopped.

These conditions were ideal for Kratch. It was dark enough not to hurt his eyes, yet light enough for him to see his prey. Ned once again led his band of warriors to the surface. Here he adjusted the Tooth in his pouch of weeds.

At the surface they heard the sounds of spouts and saw that the ships had also moved much closer.

Across the expanse of water Kratch's bulging eyes locked with the Warriors of Light. Kratch edged forward toward his intended prey. His bulbous dark gray form undulated menacingly as he drew near the terrified Warriors of Light. Kratch would finally have his chance to destroy his nemesis Megadon, by killing them. The Warriors of Light lay frozen at the surface, spellbound and indecisive as they watched Kratch's approach. They looked to Ned for instructions, but he couldn't utter a word.

A few hundred yards away Flop watched as a whaling boat quietly approached a sleeping calf and her mother. Ned had told them of this practice and how they would harpoon the calf first, and when the mother tried to save her child they would then kill her too.

Flop broke from his companions, and with an unusual burst of speed, made a break for the calf. The Warriors of Light couldn't react fast enough to tell Flop he was also swimming directly toward Kratch.

With harpoon raised, the boat steadied over the whales. The cow and her calf awoke too late to make an orderly escape from the whaler. The boat was close enough to take the calf and the harpoon just left the hand of the harpooner when a massive body of whale came breaching from the deep.

Flop's first breach earned him a harpoon in the side. He fell hard to the surface with a guttural moan of pain; the sound penetrated the air and water. The harpooner was ecstatic, thinking he had just made the catch of the day, a forty ton humpback.

Flop lay rolling in pain as the whaler's yelled instructions in a foreign language. The whalers were unaware of the bulging eyes that filled the scene very close to the injured Flop. What the harpoon hadn't achieved yet, Kratch was planning to finish.

Kratch neared Flop as Ned began to fumble for the Tooth. A sudden jerk sent Ned into a full three hundred and sixty degree spin. Ned was reeling and as he recovered his balance all he saw was a ten foot dorsal cutting the water with incredible speed. It was Kila. It seems his fear of life wasn't as strong as his love for Flop. He wrestled the Tooth free from Ned.

As Kratch lifted his razor sharp flipper to cut Flop in two, his eyes never left the pained and helpless eyes of his victim. Before Kratch could deliver his deadly blow, he was rammed just under his raised right flipper as the sharp Tooth and the pointed jaw of Kila penetrated his unnaturally evil heart. Kratch winced in agony and somehow found the strength to raise the flipper one more time to strike Flop.

To the horror of the Warriors of Light it appeared Kila had missed the target. Kratch made a vicious face and a loud screech to emphasize the blow he was about to deliver. He reached the height of the desired angle to finish off Flop when a band of clear and long tentacles reached nowhere and caught the flipper and held it tight. It was the Jellyfish Wizard.

Kratch looked over his side in amazement to see the smiling face of his one time ally pulling him away from Flop. Suddenly, Kratch made a deep gasp. The Jellyfish Wizard looked into the sky and released Kratch rapidly and swam to the side of Kila and Flop. He quickly wrapped the two whales in his tentacles and dragged them away from Kratch.

Kratch was still and wheezing in pain. In the horizon, the clouds opened to intense light at the very north, south, east and west of each position. Like a gigantic fuse, a stream of diamond white light burned intensely across the sea to intersect with the Tooth. Kratch's eyes bulged to the heavens and he let out one final shriek of pain as Kratch exploded into a million coal sized chunks of grey meat.

It appeared that Kila's strike under his flipper had found the intended target after all.

The whalers were covered with the remains of Kratch. The stench of his flesh was so awful that the whalers went below decks to escape the foul odor in the air and clean up.

The Jellyfish Wizard released Kila and Flop in time to see the results of their long mission. The Wizard excused himself to get to the cave to help free the Millennium Angel and find his sons. Ned and the others could only nod in thanks to the fast retreating Wizard.

Flop's painful look was temporarily replaced with one of joy over the death of Kratch. Kila moved in close to the side of Flop. The two friends looked to each other in triumph and with pride. Then they began to weep. Kila, the cowardly Killer Whale had moved beyond his fear, motivated by the love of his friend. Now he was the greatest of heroes, the one who defeated Kratch.

Flop lay near death and the Warriors of Light gathered round, holding him at the surface. They were all crying. The whalers began to filter back onto the deck and their captain eased the boat closer to the gathering of whales and Lonah. No one left Flop's side. The whaling boat was as close as it could get and the harpooner took his stance over the assembled whales. With harpoon in hand, the whaler lifted it to his shoulder and paused as he heard a human voice address him.

"Mr. Whaler," the little voice asked. "Haven't you caused enough pain today and for all time by killing these magnificent whales?"

The whaler looked down at the dolphin-boy with absolute astonishment. He slowly placed his harpoon on the deck and listened.

"You have wounded a hero of the ocean today, one who has helped save our planet from the forces of evil. You have, in the past, killed mothers, fathers and babies. All of these animals share the same air and sea as you," Ned implored. "Yet you choose to kill them. You have destroyed families and caused much grief. These whales love their young as we do. They don't hurt anything or anyone, and they share our world as brothers and sisters of harmony. I beg you to please stop this carnage."

The whaler could see the pain and caring in Ned's face and in the gathering of whales. Seeing Lonah, it was obvious that even a great white shark shared this concern for the sanctity of life, hugging the side of the bleeding Flop. Perhaps this boy dolphin was right ... or was he? The whaler looked to the captain who sat alongside the harpooner as he listened to Ned.

A long moment passed and the whaler lifted the harpoon holding it over his head. It appeared they didn't care to listen. The harpooner leaned over the bow of the boat taking aim at the gathering of whales and Lonah. He raised the harpoon and thrust it straight down into open water.

All of them closed their eyes with the expectation of getting run through by the harpoon. Ned opened his eyes when he heard the harpoon splash, looking around to see who was dying nearby. What Ned saw instead were Kila, Lonah, and Eccoh all looking for the same thing. The harpooner laughed at them and pointed to the sinking harpoon that was twisting downward into the depths of the sea.

"I'm sorry about your friend, the humpback," the whaler told them. "We have decided never to pursue another whale again."

Sounds of radio chatter filled the decks. Ned asked the harpooner what was going on. "It is the commander of this fleet," he said, sweeping his palm to indicate the location of the many boats that surrounded the whales.

"He has told them all to go home — for good."

Ned and the others watched as the boats began to leave. The boat nearest them backed off as well, leaving the whales in peace for all time. "We have stopped the whaling!" Eccoh proclaimed

As a smaller boat approached from the distance, Eccoh rode high off the water on her tail to observe it. Ned did the same as Eccoh and could see the boat was one he knew well.

It was the *Krill*.

Flop was losing a great deal of blood as the *Krill* pulled along side the Warriors of Light. Ned's excitement at seeing his father would have to wait. His friend, Flop, needed help. Ned relayed the details of Flop's dilemma to his dad and Conway. Ned's father looked on in astonishment at seeing the dolphin next to the boat with his son's voice. One look into the eyes of that dolphin was all he needed to know that it was Ned. How Ned ever became a dolphin was a question to be answered at a later time. Ned was frantic with calls for help.

Within minutes the two professors were both in wet suits pulling buckets of supplies through the water to Flop. "Ned," Professor Miller barked. "We need the teeth of that Killer Whale to pull the harpoon loose."

Indeed, the harpoon that hit Flop was still embedded in his side. Kila grasped the handle of the harpoon with his bared teeth. The crunch of wood and metal filled the air as he tugged the harpoon free. Flop moaned in agony. The Warriors of Light watched as the harpoon sunk toward the bottom.

Professors Conway and Miller had Flop turn to his side. They then applied an enormous wad of gauze, along with huge white pads they used for oil spills. Large handfuls of lard-like disinfectant helped fill the gaping wound. A thin line of rope secured the dressing over his body and soon he was all patched up.

Professor Miller was famous for having industrial sized portions of everything on board. Luckily, that included medicines and giant gauze pads. This time he was able to patch and save a whale, not to mention begin to heal the wounds of his estranged son.

In a moment, he did something he hadn't been able to do for years, win back the love of his boy.

"Flop will be all right," Professor Miller assured the grateful Warriors of Light. Professor Conway found himself being embraced by Lonah. His surprise and initial fear amused them all. There in the water, Ned's father hugged his son and told him of his love and of his sorrow and his deep remorse for how he had treated Ned.

Eccoh, Kila, and Lonah swam along with Flop who showed signs of recovery immediately. He managed to swim slowly away from the site of his meeting with Kratch and the harpooner. Before Flop went very far, he told Kila he loved him. Kila blushed.

Chunks of Kratch still floated around them. A strong

wind from the south slowly began to disperse the foul flesh into the far off sea. Ned swam to Kila and held him close, thanking him for delivering the crucial blow to Kratch.

Suddenly bursts of neon green light penetrated the oceans of the world. A light illuminated everything in the ocean, one powerful light that would never be seen again. This signaled the end of Kratch's evil reign, a new beginning for all ocean dwellers.

General Slash, Tentacle and the Wizard were gathered at the cave that imprisoned the Millennium Angel. The Wizard became illuminated in a rainbow of neon colors and the cave lit up as if it were on fire. The ends of the cave blew off as if shot by cannons and the light filled the cave.

Bullycudas by the hundred's began to arrive. They, too, had escaped Kratch, and came to help disassemble the cave. They all went at it taking coral and peeling the cave open to let the Millennium Angel out. When the job was complete, the light in the tunnel became blinding in all directions. The Bullycudas, Tentacle and General Slash backed off as they watched the most beautiful Angel emerge from the cave.

Awakened by the light and the call of the All Knowing, she came forth.

The Millennium Angel was magnificent. Her soft white wings of gold and magenta flowed in the waters as she made her way gracefully to the surface. Then like magic, she took to the air. They gazed upward and were filled with wonder as they realized a new dawn was upon the oceans, and each one was grateful for the role they played in this emergence of new light on Earth.

The neon green flash also gave Megadon the news of Kratch's defeat. Megadon's hope for the world was renewed. He began to swim in the direction of the new energy permeating the seas. As if by magic he found himself face to face with the Jellyfish Wizard.

He was stunned and ready to fight when the Wizard spoke. "Wait, Megadon, I have come to lead you to your son and also to rescue mine. Kratch has held my sons as he has yours. Trust me Megadon, I know your pain and of your desire to see Naw. Follow me!"

Megadon could sense that the invitation was genuine and he followed the luminous Wizard.

Megadon and the Wizard were poised over the dwelling of Kratch. The two powerful leaders made their way into the depths of Kratch's foul cave to find their sons. Not a single Bullycuda stood guard. Sharks by the hundreds arrived to see Naw. A few calls from Megadon in the dark helped them to locate Naw and the three jellyfish quickly.

Naw burst out of the opening of Kratch's hole into the freedom of the open sea. It was finally over. The great leader swam to his son as their eyes met. Megadon held Naw close to him for a long moment. The Jellyfish Wizard was also entangled in a loving embrace with his three sons.

An armada of grey dorsal fin's cut the waters making way to the grounds of the whales and Ned. The Millennium

Angel flew over the whales, and as she neared Flop she lowered her magnificent wing. A glow of white light surrounded Flop's wound. He was healed instantly by the magic of her love. His bandage fell away and Flop moved from the others and began to breach — one after the other. His astounded friends witnessed these miracles.

While Flop breached, the Millennium Angel blessed the Warriors of Light with her magic. They, too, were filled with her healing touch and the energy of her love and gratitude. By defeating Kratch they opened the way for the Millennium Angel to fulfill her destiny. The Angel flew over Lonah and then Eccoh and Kila. Each of them she stroked with her wing. Her show of gratitude complete, she flew off to begin her work on earth.

Looking in the distance, Eccoh could see dolphins by the thousands creating a white water horizon with their animated jumps and expert swimming. The dolphin's curiosity explored the origin of the searing energy that had filled the oceans.

A loud and annoying buzz filled Eccoh's ears and suddenly disappeared. She had never heard such sound before. Then the clicks and whistles of the dolphins filled her every fiber. The Millennium Angel had fulfilled her life long dreams! She released a sound of delight delivered from her tail to her snout. It was indeed the sound that dolphins made. At last she could echolocate and hear the other dolphins.

Lonah's eyes were riveted on an amazing sight in the

opposite direction. As far as the eye could see, the waters were filled with tall, flowing dorsal fins belonging to thousands of sharks. He knew his father was leading the way. Lonah began to swim in toward him, but stopped. A strange feeling filled his mouth that felt like fingers poking his gums. When he moved his tongue over the sensitive spots he nearly cut himself on the new teeth that were filling his mouth: rows and rows of them! Now he could take his rightful place among the sharks. This was another miracle in a day filled with miracles.

Kila and Flop were just enjoying each other, playing a game of chase — totally consumed by the joy of the moment and their love of life. Undoubtedly, these two whales would now be welcome with any whales, anywhere.

It seemed the entire ocean was coming to the celebration. Ned swam off to his father. At first the reunion was cumbersome, since they had developed a past filled with emotional conflict. But the past couldn't stop the dammed up emotion the father felt over seeing his son again. The two swam to one another and embraced for a long moment. Ned was teary eyed, as was his father.

The two moved back to observe the other and Ned said the most magical words a father hear.

"I love you dad."

Professor Miller told Ned how much he loved him, and that he wished to start over and have him home with him.

"Dad," Ned asked. "I have to think this over. I have a new life here with the Warriors of Light. Please, can you give me a moment?"

"Of course son. I'll wait for you."

Ned left his father and gathered with the Warriors at the bottom. He held Eccoh closely, as Kila, Flop, and Lonah all formed a circle. As they assembled, Ned's eyes connec-ted with the eyes of the others. In a haze of emotion, he composed himself before addressing them.

First he turned to Kila. "Kila, whenever I think of you, I will always remember the terrified and rejected whale that refused to join us at the Ocean Haven. I'll never forget when you barely made it into the mouth of the great Blue Whale before we were dragged to the ritual of the shark's feast. You lived in fear of life, and that fear filled your days and nights. I didn't know if you would survive our journey, but your deep rooted love helped you discover a courageous heart. That was what killed Kratch and, better yet, saved Flop. Your love for Flop was more powerful than your fear of death. You are this adventure's greatest hero. I will always love you Kila, and I will miss you dearly."

Ned was quick to move on to Flop. "Flop, what can I say to one who saved my life and risked a harpoon for the sake of saving a baby whale? With Kratch only yards away you were willing to sacrifice your life for the unsuspecting mother and her calf. You were never able to breach, but when it mattered most you soared higher than any whale I've ever seen. Thank you for your leadership and devotion to the Warriors of Light."

Flop acknowledged Ned's words with a grateful nod.

Lonah was next in line. He floated along side Flop, his chest puffed out.

"Lonah, you couldn't live up to your father's expect-ations. In your world of magnificent hunters and bold great whites you were alone; a misfit. Having no teeth made you less than all the others. Your courage and creativity are all the teeth you'll ever need. No shark could ever be a greater champion to the Light than you Lonah.

"After all, it was your plan to fill the holes of the Giant Worms with the bone of the Blue Whale. And, it was you who risked the possible harpoon of the fishermen to save Eccoh and me from the fishermen. I will always draw from your brilliance and leadership, and I know you will remain one of the greatest of Great Whites — one deeply loved by many grateful whales."

Lonah opened his tooth filled mouth with a smile that sparked a chuckle from the others. But the gesture spoke volumes to Ned of Lonah's appreciation for the heart felt words Ned had delivered to him.

At last Ned turned to Eccoh. He was choked with emotion. "Eccoh, my sweet love," he said. "You were an in-spiration to us all with your courage and sense of purpose. When you refused to stay at the Haven, none of us could imagine our world without you. Your determination to seek a better life and your love brought us together as one. You, who could not hear the others of your kind made us hear the most important message of all — a message about the power of love. The love I have shared with you has helped me find myself. For this I will always love you more than life itself. You gave a desolate and lonely boy hope and helped me find my spirit. And you found the Tooth."

Ned paused and struggled to find the words that came next. "My father wants me to come back with him. It is with great reluctance that I plan to leave all of you. I love you Eccoh," Ned told her as he swam to hold her.

They both embraced, knowing that their destinies would put them on separate paths.

At last, Eccoh spoke to Ned on behalf of the group. "Ned, you've been our leader and our dearest friend. If it weren't for your quick thinking and brave heart, our journey would have ended at the feast of the sharks. You've made us believe in ourselves and for that we hold a love for you that cannot be measured. Even though you will join your father when we all leave here today, you'll never leave us. Not ever. You will always be in our hearts, encircled by our love. So, goodbye, my love," Eccoh whispered, and kissed Ned on the cheek.

She turned to swam with the oncoming dolphins, looking back longingly at Ned until she was out of sight.

Lonah's father was waiting at the surface. Without a word he embraced Ned and surfaced to be with the boy's proud father.

Flop and Kila squeezed Ned between them. "We won't say goodbye," Flop told Ned. "You'll be back. We whales know things, and this I know. Go to your father.

"Oh, and, by the way — we love you."

Next Kila spoke up. "Thank you for having faith in me, Ned, I will miss you terribly. I too, will always love you, goodbye Ned."

Kila and Flop moved to the surface, and shortly Ned heard a loud splash above. He looked up to see them both breaching. The two didn't stop until the sun set that night.

At the surface, a celebration was in full swing. The ocean's creatures swam and played beneath a rainbow filled sky. Megadon and Naw had arrived, and eagerly sought out Ned's company.

Megadon came to Ned, smiling, exposing an enormous mouth full of gigantic teeth. This smile said everything to Ned.

"Come here, Ned," Megadon insisted. "My son and I are reunited because of you and your strange collection of Warriors. The Angel and the Oceans of Light have been saved. You are all heroes and will always be treated as such. Do you intend to stay?"

"No, Megadon," Ned replied. "I have chosen to go back to the world of land and be with my father."

Naw spoke up. "Believe me Ned, we understand." He nudged his doting father.

"Well, Ned," Megadon said in an odd tone. "Before you swim off, there is something I have to tell you. In our world we have the obligation and the privilege of joining the All Knowing when our time is over here on Earth. It is a moment of great honor for all of us and my time is near.

"Naw will take his rightful place to lead this wonderful ocean world, and I will intentionally swim to my final resting place where I will release my soul to the great unknown. When I do, this body will start to disappear and eventually my jawbone will be exposed to the world. You, my boy will have a vision of this event in a dream. It will be imperative that you come find me in that final resting place after you have it.

"Act quickly," Megadon said, "as my jawbone will be exposed to the sun. Written on it will be the secret of the Universe. It will be for you to deliver this secret to the world. *You* are the chosen messenger."

This information dumbfounded Ned, but before he could respond, Naw and Megadon disappeared.

Ned began digesting this news as he came to the surface. As he looked up, there was Dawinn, hovering above him. Suddenly, Dawinn came toward him at blinding speed. A ball of light entered Ned's forehead and sent a jolt throughout his body. Ned opened his eyes and saw that Dawinn and the rainbow were gone. The world looked and felt different, and as Ned looked at himself, there he was, a boy swimming in the ocean. His father was waiting nearby to welcome him home. There was a churning in Ned's soul that made one thing clear to him: the quest he had pursued after consuming the Ocean Potion was far from over.

In fact it has just begun.

EPILOGUE

The Millennium Angel spread her love and kindness to the planet, and Her magical ways caused a wave of spiritual connectedness, filling the hearts and consciousness of people with the power of the love for the All Knowing. A sense of renewed love for one another filled the world and the new Millennium began with a great light, outshining the darkness.

The *Krill* returned to a hero's welcome as the news of Drs. Miller and Conway's discoveries spread. Reporters from every part of the country came to hear about the mysteries of how whales migrate had been proven. They were also very excited that the whalers had miraculously called it quits. There was great interest in the story told by whalers of a boy dolphin. The professors said nothing.

Ned was along the port side of the *Krill*, performing the duties of deck hand as he had in the past. At the dock, Ned tossed the line onto the cleat on his first try like an expert. Once again, Professor Blanchard was waiting to catch the line, only this time he gave Ned a very wide grin, accompanied by a look of respect that made Ned's heart pound with joy.

The professor was invited to lecture internationally about how the baleen whales formulated the images of coastline and underwater cliffs and mountains to find their way to the mating and feeding grounds each season. Ned encouraged him to go, but the professor refused so he could spend the time with Ned. They discovered a great deal in common, and the professor was training Ned to become the captain of the *Krill*. He turned out to be an excellent skipper and was looking forward to the next research mission with the college. Ned and his father found the love they had lost when his mother died.

Ned began to dream of jungles and vast green forests, with wild birds and giant bats. At first he discounted them as the workings of his active imagination. Then one morning at the dock he saw Dawinn fly overhead. He knew what this meant, and that night he was afraid to go to sleep. Finally, exhaustion lulled him into the realm of dreams.

There he saw Megadon and Naw swimming side by side. Ned could see the coastline and green lush forest of his previous dreams. Suddenly, he felt an enormous jolt. In that same moment he had a vision of Megadon beaching on a sandy shore. Ned could feel himself rustling in his bed to find a comfortable position just as he envisioned Megadon turning and resting for good in the sand.

Soon, he felt the release of Megadon's spirit. It was like the release of a great bird that floated free, soaring upward. Ned felt the hand of the All Knowing gather the soul of Megadon to Him and he experienced a rush of emotion, peace, joy and bliss — feelings that words cannot describe. Ned opened his eyes and raced to the bedroom window. He looked up to see a comet streaking across the starry night.

The comet cut across the full moon like a laser beam, and disappeared into the vastness of space.

Megadon was home at last.

Ned, in his sleep state was still locked into this bizarre nocturnal fantasy. He reasoned that the dream wasn't real and he would awake free of the burden which Megadon had warned him of.

Then he heard a voice. He heard the faint voice of Megadon summoning Ned to hurry to his side. "The secret Ned," the voice said. "Find the secret."

Ned jumped from his bed, looked out to the water and listened to the gentle lapping of water on the shoreline. He quietly packed his knapsack, wrote a note to his father and walked out the front door.

The search for Megadon's abandoned body and the secret of the universe had begun!

Look for Book Two of the *Millennium Angel* trilogy

THE SECRET

Join Ned in the second book of the Millennium Angel trilogy and follow his exploits as he searches the shorelines of the Amazon in search of Megadon's jawbone.

Cutting a path to the beach he hopes will lead to the great jaw of Megadon, Ned encounters many roadblocks and dilemmas with the native inhabitants of the Amazon River Basin. If he makes it before the encroaching total eclipse, he will receive the mystical secret the world is waiting to know!

For updates on *The Secret* and
other works by Bob Wilds, log on to:

THEANGELOF2000.COM

Millennium Angel

The Millennium Angel is sent to Earth on a mission to heal the planet. The Dark Forces of the Ocean capture her while she awaits the New Age. Given the task of saving her are a cowardly Killer Whale, a Dolphin that cannot hear or speak 'Dolphinese', a hapless Humpback, a toothless Great White Shark, and Ned, a boy whose self-worth has been battered by a condescending father.

In a magical way, these unlikely heroes come to battle unfriendly foes.

Passing through territories where danger raises its head at every turn, they learn valuable lessons about Life, and find that the simple act of faith in themselves was all the magic they ever needed.

About the Author

Millennium Angel is the first book in a trilogy. In each story, the characters are challenged to save a certain place in our world. Issues of consciousness and healing are incorporated to create a blend of magic and discovery. I hope this story brings you as much joy to read as it did for me in writing it. — *Bob Wilds*

Bob is a naturalist aboard a whale-watching vessel out of Barnstable Harbor, Cape Cod, Massachusetts. He currently resides in Cotuit with his wife Nancy, and two dogs: Annie and Buck

Price: $7.50